Other Titles by Edie Ramer

Christmas Redemption

Love & Murder, Book 5

Edie Ramer

Blue Walrus Books

Published by Blue Walrus Books

ISBN: 978-1-939328-33-5

Cover design by EJR Digital Art
Copy-editing by Blue Otter Editing
Proofreading by Judicious Designs
Formatting by Author E.M.S.

Published in the United States of America.

"One can never have enough socks," said Dumbledore. "Another Christmas has come and gone and I didn't get a single pair. People will insist on giving me books."

~J.K. Rowling, *Harry Potter and the Sorcerer's Stone*

Acknowledgments

Thank you to the many authors whose books about Christmas I've enjoyed, whether they were children's books, romance, or murder. Romance fits a season when your heart is open to love. Murder is the opposite of love. A coldness of the heart. The yin, the yang, the food, the presents, the romance, and the murder.

And thank you to the readers who, like me, enjoy a little suspense in your Christmas fiction.

One

"WARNING TO ANY Michiganders who might be listening. First, you had to watch out for the water. Now, you have to watch out for a modern-day Bonnie and Clyde. Yep. You heard me right. They change their hair color. They change their cars. They change their names. And you know what else they do, peeps?"

In the Subaru's front passenger seat, Sylvia looked at Nate, her eyebrows up. His eyes were on the traffic, but he must have felt her gaze because he smiled, his cheeks pouching up. Her slightly chubby teddy bear with his curly gray hair, protuberant nose, and ready smile.

"Aren't you sorry now that you didn't listen to NPR?" he asked.

She laughed. After living in a small town in Door County, Wisconsin, for the first fifty-three years of her life, she relished her new life in Madison with its concerts, plays, art exhibits, and often listening to National Public Radio. Still, it felt good to be going home for Christmas. This Christmas would be tamer than the last, she was sure, and glad for it.

1

"They murder." The DJ's smooth voice regained her attention. "You heard me right. I said murder, and that's what they do."

Sylvia supposed the DJ meant to be humorous, but she shuddered, and it wasn't because of the twelve-degree temperature outside or the meteorologist's snow warnings. She'd had enough of murder, and none of it had been funny. Especially since some of the murders had involved her.

She had killed three people and hadn't been caught.

Yet.

She planned on the *yet* to mean *never ever*.

At least she hadn't killed maliciously. Except, perhaps, once.

She'd been younger then. Ice-cold outside; boiling hot inside.

Crying inside.

Screaming inside.

Feeling like the world's biggest fool.

Worrying about what would happen to her son.

Worrying about what would happen to her.

There had been no prenuptial agreement. Her cheating, drinking, deadbeat husband would have claimed half of the bed-and-breakfast she'd grown up in. The bed-and-breakfast that had been in her family for generations.

And from Charley...? He would have given her nothing. Not even child support for Chuck, their son.

Even now the memories made her clench her teeth tightly. Forcing her jaw to relax, she reminded herself that Chuck was thirty-one, had recently started a business that was helping artists in the community, and was engaged to a wonderful and talented woman. Every time he looked at Raine, his face lit up.

A big difference from his father. At Charley's wake, she'd overheard one of his drinking buddies say, "Charley was always up for a fun time, but I'm not surprised that he's gone. If any man was born to die with a bullet in his cheating heart, that man was Charley."

Perhaps she should have waited for someone else to kill him, but she was never the type to wait for other people to do her dirty work.

And the other two murders...well, there were reasons for those, too.

In one case, she had saved lives.

Her other victim had ruined lives.

But Charley's murder... As much as she told herself that he had deserved to die, it haunted her.

Her hands shook, and she curled her fingers into her palms. She was not the same person now. She needed to let go of the past. She needed to be happy. She needed to forgive herself, although after more than two decades, the hurt was still there. A raw wound that had never healed.

She took a deep breath. She was just here for the Christmas holidays. She and Nate would be staying until after New Year's while Chuck and Raine visited Raine's sister and her sister's baby in Santa Barbara.

When this holiday was over and Sylvia and Nate returned to Madison, Sylvia planned to work on forgiving herself and finally unclenching the closed fist that was squeezing her heart so tightly.

For a beginning, she could let her heart beat steadily.

She could breathe deeper and slower.

She could accept Nate's marriage proposal.

She could allow herself to be happy.

Sitting with her back straight, she felt better now that she had a plan. A goal. Until the time was right to put her thoughts into actions, she would enjoy the holiday and help give the couple who had booked a suite at the bed-and-breakfast a Christmas they would never forget.

The DJ promised to play the new Adele song after the commercial. Julian reached forward to lower the volume, then turned to the driver. "You know what I like most about Wisconsin?"

"Cheese." Avery steered the car along the Upper Michigan road, the heater on high, snow and pine trees on both sides of the country road. "And beer."

He glanced sideways. One thing Avery did well was drive. His mother had preferred to be driven, and so did he.

And Avery had money. He liked that. Liked that very much.

He took after his mother that way, too.

And Avery liked going down on him. Another thing he liked very much.

A memory flashed in his mind.

He was ten years old, hearing guttural sounds

coming from his mother's bedroom. Sounds like someone was dying.

He hurried down the hall. The door was open, and he stopped and stared. His mother and Carl, his second stepfather, were naked on the huge bed, his mother kneeling between Carl's legs, her head down.

Watching them, Julian sucked in his breath, nervous and excited and mesmerized.

Carl's croaks became louder and louder, until he let loose with a roar, his hips slamming up and down between his mother's hands, smashing against her face. Julian was still staring when his mother rolled off of his stepfather and flopped down on the bed next to him, the side closest to the hallway.

Then she turned her head and looked at him, her eyes dark.

A small smile appeared on her face. She opened her mouth, and he could see the shininess inside. He was old enough to know what that was.

He ran to his room, closing the door, shoving his hand down his pants.

In the car, he shut down those thoughts.

Even before that night, he'd known he was different from other kids his age. He'd celebrated the difference. The others were lemmings. He was a shark.

His mother had been a shark, too. He'd give that to her. The kind of shark who liked to bite her son. Showing him she was the one in charge.

Avery was a shark, too, but a smaller shark. A baby shark. He was the biggest shark. The smartest one. So when Avery said foolish things, which she often did, he let them go. After all, he never had liked women with brains.

Women like his mother, who was living in Greece with husband number four. He hadn't seen her since she moved to Manhattan with husband number three when he was seventeen, but she sent him a Christmas card every year.

"What I like about Wisconsin," he said finally, "is that no one will expect us to strike there."

Avery giggled again. He sat back with a half smile, dismissing his memories. They were part of yesterday and had no meaning to him. Shakespeare had been wrong. The past wasn't prologue. The past was dust.

Santa was coming to the town of Trouble Bay, and Julian was going to get a very big Christmas present. He knew that because he was giving the present to himself.

He touched the car's digital screen, switching to another station. Then he sat back, the corners of his lips curling as he listened to his favorite holiday song, "You're a Mean One, Mr. Grinch."

Two

THE CAT WAS scared and cold. So cold it hurt. She didn't know how long she'd been outside. The barn she was in had fallen down last night, blocking her from her sisters, her brother, and her mom, who had run off as she'd cowered in the corner of the barn.

Now she was alone, her paws cold. Her face cold. Her eyes cold. Everything cold.

She had finally climbed over the rotten boards and tried to follow the others, but the paw indents had disappeared. Cat's nose was cold, too, so maybe that's why she couldn't smell them. It felt like the gusting wind was blowing right through her. Maybe that's why she couldn't hear the snow crunching beneath their paws. Maybe they were too far away.

She'd made it into the town. Maybe her mom and the others were sheltering in one of the buildings on each side of the street. She meowed. If she meowed loudly enough, maybe her mom would call out to her, saying, *I'm here, little one! I'm here!*

But though she screeched as loud as she

could, her mom didn't meow back. No sisters or brother, either. Only a few cars made noises, driving slowly down the street. Cat knew what cars were. Something to avoid. Up to now, she had run faster than the cars. Too fast and nimble for any car to catch her.

But not now, with the pads of her paws so frozen it hurt to walk on them. So frozen it scared her.

A car was coming now, slowing and turning.

Something else was happening, too.

A large door on a building was rolling up to the building top.

The car drove into the big opening.

She raced after the car as fast as she could, every step a jolt, like needles sticking into the pads of her paws. The door was coming down now. Fast. Too fast. She scooted inside just before the door banged down, just missing the end of her tail. With a squeak, she dived into the nearest corner.

There was another car in the garage, along with other stuff. Humans always had *stuff*. She knew that much about humans, and she didn't want to know more.

The car doors opened, and she hunched in the corner. Cat was smaller than her brother and sisters, and she needed to make herself look even smaller. Her heart beating too fast, she backed up farther into the corner, right into *things*. Human things, with long wooden handles and hard stuff on the bottoms.

Hunkering down in the small space, she shivered from fear and cold. Inside her chest, her heartbeat raced, and she hunched down a bit more.

A man walked past her and opened the back of the car. The other human, a woman—Cat could tell from her scent—came around the other side. If the woman glanced down, she would see Cat. Instead, the woman looked at the man, laughing at something he said, though Cat heard a sad note in her laughter.

They both lifted boxlike things out of the car. The man set his box next to his feet. As he did, the woman's box slid out of her grip and crashed onto the floor.

Cat squealed.

The woman twisted around faster than the man. They both stared straight at her. They both saw her.

But they were human, and Cat knew she was faster than any human.

Leaping forward, she extended her claws. Out of the corner of her eye, she saw the woman lunging toward her, faster than Cat had thought a human could move. Cat landed on the cold, hard floor, and a sharp pain stabbed through her paws and up into her legs.

For a second, she paused, and in that second, the woman swooped down and swept Cat into her arms, pulling Cat against her chest.

Cat squawked and squirmed, but the woman gripped her too tightly for Cat to wiggle away, and her clothes were too thick for Cat's claws to penetrate. Something covered the woman's hands, too. Cat could feel them on her back. Warm. The woman's front was warm, too.

The man opened a small door on the side of the building. The woman said something to him as she rushed out into the cold. Squished against the woman's front, Cat felt the woman's every step and every bounce.

Another building cast a shadow on them. The man and woman hurried toward it. Cat screeched loud and hard, wiggling as much as she could with the arms holding her tightly. To no avail. The woman clung to her as if she would never let her go.

Cat fought. She screeched. She squirmed. But the woman didn't let her go for what seemed like too long a time until another door opened, and Cat could feel warm air shoot out at them. The woman surged forward, inside this new building. The man spoke, closing the door.

Cat stopped her screeching. *Where was she?* Cat had thought her heart was beating fast before, but now it was beating three times as fast. Too fast to even allow her to screech.

Maybe this was another barn, and the woman was going to leave her here. If only the woman would release her, Cat wouldn't be so scared. The woman's grip didn't hurt, but Cat didn't trust humans. They were big and loud and not to be trusted.

The woman's grip loosened, and quicker than a flying hawk, Cat wiggled, her paws pushing against the human's front.

The next second she was on the floor and running as fast as she could. She didn't know what she was running from or where she was running to, but she wasn't going to stop.

After all, she was Cat. Small like a rabbit but fast like the wicked winter wind.

Three

WHILE NATE BROUGHT their luggage inside, Sylvia found an empty box in the basement. She hurried upstairs with the box, then asked Nate to bring in the bag of sand they kept in the corner of the garage. His eyebrows quirked up.

"If the driveway is icy," she said, "we sprinkle sand on it. Right now, the sand will have to do double duty."

"Ah." He zipped up his jacket and turned toward the doorway. "That makes sense."

Nate left for the garage again as she headed to the kitchen. She opened a can and dumped tuna into a small China bowl with a bluebird on the side. She heard Nate return, huffing a bit, as she found a matching bowl for the water.

An image in her mind of the small, ginger-striped tabby eating and drinking out of her bluebird bowls made her smile.

She hesitated over leaving the bowls in the kitchen or the hallway, then deciding on the cloakroom. The cat was afraid of her and Nate. It would feel more comfortable eating in the cloakroom. A safe place. In the instant before

Sylvia had grabbed the cat, she'd taken in the smallness of the cat's trembling body. She'd seen the look of starvation. Even with her gloves on, she'd felt the cat's bones and the slightness. She doubted if the cat weighed more than a few pounds.

In the cloakroom a moment later, she noted the cardboard box against the back wall that Nate had already filled with a few inches of sand. She set down the bowls closer to the hallway, then headed to the living room. The decor was a muted elegance. People often told her that it suited her style, but they were wrong. This classic style was what their guests expected. She preferred a cleaner, more modern style.

She made a beeline to the storage bench by the living room staircase and took out a blue velveteen blanket that had always been one of her favorites. After putting the cushions back on the bench, she hurried back to the cloakroom. She set the folded blanket against the inner wall, then fluffed it up so it would be more cozy for the cat.

The bowls looked untouched. Frowning, she strode to her bedroom in the back to unpack.

"Did you find the cat?" Nate was putting the few clothes he'd brought in the top dresser drawer.

"It's still hiding," she said.

He tilted his head and held out his arms to her. "Come here. I can tell you're worried."

Not saying a word, she stepped toward him like she was a homing pigeon and he was her home. With his arms around her, his gut stuck out slightly into her slimmer stomach—and she didn't care. She didn't judge. Her late husband, with all his perfect looks, had never made her feel this cared for. This loved. This precious.

"What now?" he asked. "Hungry?"

"I'm still full," she said, her head still on his shoulder. They'd stopped off in Green Bay for an early dinner that they'd finished less than an hour ago. They'd both had tomato soup and a chicken wrap and had shared a slice of key lime pie.

"You want to cuddle?" His voice was low and caring, but she sighed.

She felt sad today. Sad for the cat. Sad for her wasted life. Sad for the mistakes she'd made. No matter how often she told herself to move on, she was stuck in the past. She suspected that committing murder did that to people—at least the ones with a conscience. But feeling sorry for herself didn't make anything better.

"Sounds wonderful," she said, "but first I need to put away my clothes."

He pulled away just far enough to look into her eyes. "If you leave the unpacking until later, no one will punish you. Even if you leave it until tomorrow."

"I know." She took another step back. It was nice to be reminded that she didn't *have* to do this. But if she didn't, it would bug her. Like walking around with a small stone in her shoe. "It will only take a few minutes."

"I'll make hot chocolate," he said. "Or we can skip the hot chocolate and drink wine as we listen to Nina Simone."

"Wine is healthier than hot chocolate, but today I'll go with the chocolate."

"We're living dangerously." He grinned. "If you want to watch TV instead, that's fine with me. There's probably old Christmas movies on the different channels."

She shook her head. "I do love a good Christmas movie, but hot chocolate, Nina Simone, and cuddling on the couch with you sounds like a perfect evening."

An hour and a half later, Nate was snoring softly on the couch, his mouth slightly open, and Nina Simone was singing the same song for the third time. Sylvia pushed up from the couch, grabbed the empty mugs, and headed to the kitchen, where she rinsed out the mugs and left them in the sink. Only then did she walk softly to the cloakroom, the light from the kitchen shining into the hallway. She stood in the open doorway and saw that the tuna was gone. The water was down about a third. And the blanket had an indent, as if a small cat had curled up on it.

She didn't move for another moment, looking around the small room. She had a feeling... *There.* In the back, beneath a long coat of hers, something stopped her. Something that wasn't supposed to be there. It took a few seconds before she realized what it was. A pair of green eyes.

A smile curved her lips. *Yes.* It felt like a victory, which was silly. After all, the cat didn't know she could see it. The cat was hiding from her. The cat was afraid of her.

But it just felt *good* to help this small creature that had been on the verge of starving. The verge of freezing. One way or another, the cat had been a short time away from death.

She'd saved a life.

She scrunched down. "I see you, kitty," she murmured. "I see you, and I'll be back. I can't keep you here. I'm sorry about that. We can't keep dogs or cats here unless we know the guests don't have pet allergies. But don't worry. Tomorrow, I'll take you to a warm place with other dogs and cats. A place where you'll find humans who can love and cherish you."

The cat edged back, as if trying to flatten itself onto the bottom of the wall and blend right in. With all the shadows, Sylvia still couldn't see the cat's small body, just its green eyes.

Her knees felt the pressure from kneeling for so long, and she straightened her legs, her back still curved down so she could see those glowing eyes.

"Sleep well, kitty. Sleep warm and safe, and I hope you have good kitty dreams."

She straightened all the way. She could still smell dark chocolate from the pot in the kitchen. She needed to either put it away or warm it up. It had been a long day. Tomorrow would be longer. Christmas Eve day, and guests would be here. She should be in a holiday mood, but coming home had stirred up old memories that she'd prefer to forget.

She made a decision to warm up the hot chocolate, then bring mugs into the living room and wake up Nate. They would drink their hot chocolate, and maybe they would cuddle some more.

As she headed toward the kitchen, she realized the song playing now was "Away in the Manger."

Nate must have woken up and turned on Christmas music for her. She smiled as she listened to the song, thinking that the cloakroom was the cat's manger. A place to be safe and warm.

For more than one hundred years, this house had been a safe place for humans.

She would tell that to the guests coming tomorrow. This would be their safe place.

Four

SUNLIGHT FILLED THE hotel room as Avery came up behind Julian. "You look just like Jesus," she said.

Julian looked at himself in the hotel room mirror. This wasn't the first time Avery had mentioned the resemblance. Not in appearance like the iconic images, depicted long after his death. But Jesus had had a power inside him. A power to lead mankind. To help mankind.

So did Julian have a power inside him—the power of life and death. To allow life...or to take it away.

This time of year, the power was flaring up inside him. Stronger than ever.

Jesus had thought mankind deserved to be saved, but Julian knew that mankind was inherently evil and greedy and selfish. Too silly. Too stupid. Too easily influenced.

Avery pressed against his back, her arms sliding around his ribs to the front of his chest. At five seven, she was three inches shorter than him, and when she wore heels she was taller. He encouraged her to wear heels. He had no ego problems. He knew he was extraordinary. Unlike most people, he controlled his life.

Sometimes, he controlled the lives of others.

He smiled at the man in the mirror. The thick eyebrows and hair. The thin face with the prominent cheekbones and the thin nose. The lean but muscled body beneath the gray sweater and black jeans.

Avery's head tilted to the left as she peered at both of them in the mirror, her breasts beneath her cashmere sweater flattened against his back. She ran her hands down his chest. "Are we going to eat breakfast?"

He twisted around and slipped his hand beneath her sweater, sliding up to cup her breast, squeezing a little. "*I'm* going to eat. Take off your pants and get on the bed."

Her face brightened. "Just my pants?"

He rubbed his thumb over her nub of a nipple. "For now," he whispered. "For now."

He was feeling generous. This would be his early Christmas present to her. After breakfast, they could come back to the room, and he would fuck her. Hard and fast. The way they both liked it. With her screaming so loud that sometimes the hotel guests in the rooms next to them pounded on the walls, which made them bang each other louder and harder.

Until they were done and she would be lying in a sex stupor. But not him. He would be lying next to her, his body satisfied, his mood euphoric as he dreamed about what he was going to do next. Creating an epic tale that would make Bonnie and Clyde look like pathetic amateurs. Common criminals who'd gotten lucky—until their luck ran out in a barrage of bullets.

That wasn't going to happen to him. Not with his brilliant mind.

With a giggle, Avery hurried to the bed. He followed her more slowly. Avery wasn't the first woman who'd worshipped him. Others had before her. And when they stopped seeing him as a god...well, then he had no more use for them.

So far, Avery had been the one who adored him the longest. She was also the richest.

As long as none of this changed, he was willing to give her what she wanted.

He didn't ask for much, really, he thought as she stripped off her jeans and then her panties, giggling, her eagerness making him smile. He only asked for absolute obedience. Absolute adoration.

He saw himself as a man who took what he wanted. A man who got what he wanted.

And all he needed was...*everything.*

"I know the cat's here." Sylvia stood in the kitchen, glancing around. Just in case the cat would suddenly appear. "We've looked everywhere. I don't know where she could be hiding."

"Don't look at me." Nate sat at the table, his laptop in front of him. "The cat is obviously gifted. I wish more of my students were that ingenious."

"If we can't find her, we can't take her to the Humane Society."

Nate grinned. "I suspect that's the cat's idea. Besides, it's Christmas Eve day. It's unlikely that they're taking in strays today."

"You think this is funny, don't you?"

"I like spunk in my animals and my woman."

"Your woman? Is that what I am?" She put her hands on her hips.

"Spunk and brains." He grinned wider, as if he knew that he looked cute with laughter in his eyes and his face.

She shook her head but smiled back at him, letting go of her mix of worry and irritation. How could she be mad at the cat when its antics made them smile and laugh? She'd spent too many years living life as if every day was serious. Too many years trying to be perfect.

She didn't want to be that person any more.

"What if one of the guests is allergic?" she asked.

"Then you tell them you couldn't let the cat freeze to death, and if the cat bothers them, there's a very nice resort nearby that has lovely rooms and a view of Lake Michigan. Tell them you know the owners, and you might even wrangle a discount for them."

"If I asked August, he probably would."

Nate grinned. "And if you're worried about losing money, I'll make up the difference."

She folded her arms under her breasts. "Of course I wouldn't let you do that."

"It would be worth it to have you to myself." His right eyebrow quirked. "No students. No relatives. Just you and me, babe."

"It wouldn't be just you and me," she said,

feeling triumphant. "It will be you, me, and the cat."

He laughed and stood, the chair pushing back as he held out his arms. "The invisible cat. Come here and give me a hot holiday kiss. 'Tis the season of miracles, you know."

"I thought we were celebrating Jesus's birth?"

"I'm talking about Chanukah, which already started." He took a step toward her. "Chanukah is a festival to celebrate light over darkness. To celebrate miracles."

"And what's your miracle?" she asked her Jewish lover as he stopped inches from her.

"You. You're my miracle." He put his arms around her, and she leaned into him. Feeling as if she were coming home.

They kissed, and joy and desire rose up inside her, a warm fire getting warmer by the second.

He finally loosened his grip, lifting his lips from hers. "The bedroom?" he asked, his voice thickened.

"Yes," she whispered. "Yes."

They separated but not completely. Nate kept his arm around her shoulders as they headed into the hallway leading to her bedroom. She was glad that they didn't have far to go. She had a sudden urge to start tearing off her clothes, and she had to resist it.

"What are you thinking?" he asked.

"That I'm becoming decadent." She looked at him. "And I like it."

His eyes sparkled at her as he steered her into the room. She could feel the joy of life—of *love*—

beaming off of him, and she grew warm and moist.

They quickly undressed. She put her clothes on the chair near the door, and so did he. They stood for a moment, looking at each other, though they'd certainly seen each other plenty for the last eleven months or so. But Nate had been busy with the university, with his students, and he'd been writing notes for his screenplays and ideas for new ones.

She had kept busy, too. Taking classes and making new friends. And she and Nate had been learning to know each other better and liking what they found out.

Liking it very much.

"We're alone now," he said. "We'd better make the most of it before the guests come."

She scrambled onto her side of the bed, under the covers because it was chilly without clothes. "I'm ready."

He looked down at his erection. Grinning, he looked back up at her. "Apparently I'm ready, too."

In seconds, he was on the bed next to her, pulling the covers over him before rolling over to face her.

As they reached out to each other, a screech came from beneath the bed. They both shot up into a sitting position, just in time for Sylvia to see a tiger-striped streak whip out of the open bedroom door.

Her mouth gaping, she looked at Nate, and he looked backed at her. They both laughed at the same time, loud and long. Then he pulled her to him and kissed her. Her laughter stopped, but her joy zoomed up five notches.

Christmas really was the best time of the year.

Apparently, so was Chanukah.

Five

SHOWTIME. THE FRONT doorbell had chimed, and Sylvia took a deep breath, assuring herself that everything looked perfect. The bed-and-breakfast had been clean when they had walked in yesterday. Chuck and Raine had even decorated an evergreen tree that stood majestically in the living room in front of the large front window. Now it was up to Sylvia to take over.

Putting on her hostess smile, Sylvia opened the front door. The young woman on the other side of the door looked like a cheerleader. Blond with a big smile and long legs. The prom queen. The popular girl. The ring on her left-hand ring finger had an emerald, not a diamond. Sylvia guessed she and the man with her were in their mid- to late twenties.

The man standing at her side looked like the sexy guy every mother told her daughter not to date—even as the mother lusted over him. His hair was light brown, his height was medium, his face looked sculpted. She would be interested to see if his body under the expensive leather jacket and jeans looked sculpted, too. Not that she'd do anything about it, but as one of her friends in Madison liked to say, *There's nothing wrong with appreciating a little man candy. You don't have to want to eat it. Just looking at it is enough.*

"You must be the Stewarts," she said. "Come in."

The couple looked at each other, then her. "Not Stewart," the man said. "I'm Brad Duncan and this is Taylor. We stopped off at the gas station in Sturgeon Bay, and someone there said this was a good place to stay for Christmas."

"Are either of you allergic to cats?" Sylvia asked as frigid air seeped into the living room entrance.

"Not me," Brad said.

Taylor's eyes shined. "I *adore* cats. Do you have one?"

Sylvia stepped back, gesturing them inside. "We found a cat in the garage yesterday. More of a kitten, maybe. We're guessing between four to six months. I took it inside, planning to take it to the Humane Society, and it got away." She swept her arm out behind her. "It's somewhere in the house."

A frown puckered Taylor's forehead. "Poor kitty. What about food?"

"And water?" Brad frowned slightly, too.

"I set out water and tuna in the cloakroom," Sylvia said. "She's been drinking the water and eating the tuna. My friend is out buying real cat food right now."

"I hope I get to see it." Taylor peered up a couple inches at her boyfriend, love shining in her eyes.

Brad beamed. "My girl has a big heart."

Sylvia glanced at the snow-covered lawn behind him. The snow was still coming down. Not hard and fast but starting to stick on the road. Still okay to drive on, as long as the drivers didn't do anything stupid.

"We have suites on the second floor and the third floor." She turned her attention back to the attractive couple. "They all have Wi-Fi and a TV. The third floor suites are larger and have a whirlpool. We serve breakfast at nine a.m."

"A whirlpool." Taylor squealed and clapped her hands. She looked at him, her eyes big. "Is that okay, honey? Can we afford it?"

He shrugged. "If it will make you happy, a whirlpool it is."

Even as he said the words, Taylor shook her head. "On second thought, it's too cold for a whirlpool. I'd rather be warm and cozy with you on the second floor."

"You're sure?"

She nodded emphatically. "Positive. Nothing you say will make me change my mind."

He laughed, putting an arm around her shoulders and hugging her.

The old Sylvia might have fought the inclination to roll her eyes. This new Sylvia felt only a small inclination to throw the key at them and tell them to hurry upstairs to the suite.

Instead she invited them into the kitchen, where she opened the old-fashioned guest book and entered their names and dates. They planned to stay for two days, leaving the morning after Christmas Day. She asked for a driver's license.

Brad handed her his license, and then he gave her his credit card. As she handled the transaction, she told them they could park in the lot on the side, and that she kept the front door open for guests until ten p.m. If they weren't planning on returning by ten, they should let her know, and she would wait up for them.

She also gave them an activity guide for Trouble Bay that included a list of favorite stores, restaurants, and activities available in the winter. The list was much shorter for the winter season than in the summer—or, as the locals called it, *tourist season.* She advised them that there were more brochures and maps for Door County in the living room on the coffee table.

Since they were her only guests right now, she led the way upstairs and opened all the second-floor suites for their inspection.

"Pretty," Taylor said on the second floor, looking out the window facing the back. "I like the houses behind you. It's like a Christmas card." She twisted toward Sylvia. "Do they all decorate?"

"Most of them, though the house directly behind us just has a few lights on." She smiled, because it was nice when good things happened to good people. "The owner and his dog spend most nights at a lady friend's house."

Taylor giggled, and Brad looked at her as if she were the best thing that had happened to him.

"In summer," Sylvia said, "when the leaves on the trees sprout, you can't see the houses behind us. It's very private here. Would you like this suite?"

They agreed and asked about a place to eat.

She recommended August's resort for dinner but said the bar a few blacks down had good pub food, too.

Heading down the stairs, Sylvia could hear their giggles, despite the closed door. She felt a twinge of jealousy. It must be nice to feel so confident in love. Even now, it was hard for her to believe wholeheartedly that she could be happy with a man. That she was loveable. Charley used to say she was born with a cold beauty like the moon and had the personality of a tax collector.

No wonder their marriage hadn't worked, as he'd been born with beauty like the sun and the personality of an eternal frat boy.

But that was the past. Her future, she reminded herself, included a man who made her laugh and gave her orgasms. A man who said he loved her. And she believed him.

As long as he didn't find out the truth about her.

As she reached the last step of the staircase, the front doorbell rang again.

Six

SYLVIA LET THE new couple in. The Stewarts. They looked alike in body type, both thin in a sleek model look, and both of them with dark hair, though the man's was a brownish black and the woman's slightly lighter. They were both medium height and they wore leather jackets. She guessed they were in their late twenties. The man carried a duffel bag, and the woman had a wheeled carry-on bag.

At first glance, Sylvia wondered if they were siblings, but the man's face was sharp, his blue eyes penetrating, and the woman's face was wider, her eyes the brown of milk chocolate.

They were holding hands. Sylvia glanced down. Perhaps holding them too tightly.

She looked up again. "I'm Sylvia."

"I'm Erica." The woman gestured to the man, and the diamond on her ring finger sparkled. "He's Nolan."

Sylvia smiled politely. "Before I sign you up, I have to know whether either of you are allergic to cats."

The man's left eyebrow rose. "Neither of us are

allergic to animals, but shouldn't this be something you mention in your information?"

"Not when it's unexpected." As Sylvia explained, Erica took out her cell phone from her purse, glancing down while her husband peered around the living room. Sylvia had the feeling that Nolan was assessing the worth of every item. Her story over, she signaled to them to follow her into the kitchen. As they signed into Sylvia's guest book, the side door opened.

Sylvia and the Stewarts turned to look around as Nate stepped into the house, carrying three large plastic bags.

"Hi, honey!" Nate stood in front of the cloakroom, grinning at her, the tip of his protruding nose red from the cold, his glasses slightly fogged, and his blue-knit hat pulled down over his forehead, covering his gray hair.

She smiled back at him, then turned to the couple. Erica was once again staring at her phone, and Nolan was frowning, looking impatient.

Her hostess smile didn't falter, though she wondered why they'd come here. Neither of them even pretended to look as if they'd come to Trouble Bay to enjoy the winter wonderland getaway.

Most of her guests were pleasant, but there were always a few who came determined not to enjoy themselves. Maybe Erica and Nolan had argued on their drive here. Or, to be charitable, maybe they'd received bad news in the last few hours. Maybe one of them had found out the other was cheating on them.

Marriage was funny. Sometimes it was wonderful. Sometimes it was murder.

"I'll take you to your room." She stepped ahead of them.

Whatever emotional luggage they brought to Trouble Bay, she wasn't going to allow it to ruin her Christmas holiday.

"Baby," Nate called. "Baby, where are you?"

Coming down the stairs, Sylvia hurried her steps, feeling lighter the farther she got from the Stewarts and the closer she was to Nate.

Emotions were contagious, and she chose to focus on Nate's cheerfulness. Let the Stewarts swim in their own pool of unhappiness. She'd been plunging into that pool for a long time, and she didn't want to even dip her big toe in the toxic water anymore.

But now Nate was calling for *baby*? Was he talking about *her*?

"Little sweetie," he crooned. "You can come to me. I won't hurt you."

She slapped her hand over her mouth to hold back laughter. *The cat.* Nate was trying to lure the cat with food. Smart move, though Sylvia thought it would take time more than food.

As she neared the bottom of the staircase, she realized his voice was coming from their bedroom instead of the cloakroom.

"Look at the cat tree I bought for you," Nate was saying. "You can climb up and look out the window. Won't that be fun? Come on, baby. Come and see."

Cat tree? Look out the window?

Sylvia reached the first floor and turned. *Oh, no. Oh, no.* But even as she tried to tell herself that Nate wouldn't do what she was thinking he'd done, she had the sinking conviction that of course he would. And it wasn't *oh, no* but *hell yes.*

Laughter came from the hallway that led to her bedroom. Taylor and Brad were standing at the entrance to the hallway, though in her mind, she called them *the cheerleader and the footballer.* The cheerleader was giggling and the footballer was grinning.

Unlike the happy couple, Sylvia was *not* amused. The hallway, which led to her and her son's bedrooms, was private. She felt an urge to open the utility closet in the kitchen, grab a broom, and slam the brush end onto their perfect heads.

How *dare* they invade her privacy?

How *dare* Nate do something this silly that would tempt them to invade her privacy?

The last time someone had invaded her privacy here, the ending had not been pretty for them.

She stopped to take a deep cleansing breath, then exhaled, not feeling cleansed. Not one bit. She strode forward anyway. As she neared the couple, they turned to her.

"I'm sorry," she said, forcing herself to speak calmly instead of shrieking, "but this area is for family. Guests aren't allowed."

"Oops." Taylor giggled, then slapped a hand over her mouth.

"Sorry for intruding." Brad nodded at her, then curved his hand over Taylor's shoulder.

"And when we came downstairs," Taylor said, her eyes bright, "we saw Nate carrying the cat climber thing to the hallway. We were waiting to see if the cat would follow him in. It was just too hard to resist."

A sound brought Sylvia's attention to the bedroom as Nate stepped into the hallway, looking sheepish.

"Of course it's nearly impossible to resist." Sylvia shot a cool glance at him before she turned back to the attractive couple. "We'll try to keep temptation away from you."

"It will be hard," Taylor said. "I just love kittens. They love me, too."

"Would you like to take the cat home?" Sylvia asked.

Brad's eyes and mouth opened in an *oh crap* look.

Taylor slapped her hands together and squealed. "Say yes, Brad! You would *love* a kitten. We can keep it, can't we?"

Brad's *oh crap* look deepened.

Sylvia smirked. If he thought this was bad, wait until he had children. In a marriage, there always seemed to be one who said no and one who said yes. And guess who was the one the kid loved more than the other?

She knew this from her own marriage, though Chuck's parental preference had changed before Charley's death. By then Charley had been spending more time away from her and Chuck. When he was at home, he was often drunk or sleeping. He'd been a poor excuse for a husband, a father, and a human being.

"Please?" Taylor's voice rose and thinned, like a small child who wanted something from her daddy.

Sylvia winced. She hated it when a woman used the little-girl voice. The women she admired were equals in their marriages. And when the women held the power in the family, Sylvia admired them even more.

"No reason to decide anything now. If you don't mind..." Sylvia stepped to the side and waited for them to turn into the living room before she marched down the hallway. Once inside her bedroom, she stared at a cat climber by the window. The thing had three perches at different heights for the cat to curl up on.

"Honey, I really thought this would lure the cat in," Nate said from behind her. "I looked it up on the Internet, and it can take weeks to find a cat. Maybe months."

She turned around. "Really? I think you just want a new play pal."

"You're the only play pal I need. I'm just putting up a toy to lure a kitten." He grinned again. "The same way you lured me."

Chuckling, he pulled her to him. She automatically put her hands on his shoulders, looking at his smiling face. This time, she wasn't smiling back at him.

She knew what he meant. What he wanted. *Marriage.* But why change anything? Why the need to make choices now? They were friends and lovers, and she was happy with that. Why couldn't he be happy, too?

It wasn't that she was afraid of changes...

She closed her eyes, because she was lying to herself. She disliked changes. Especially when it came to men. She knew in her heart that Nate wasn't going to change if she married him. She knew he would love and cherish her.

Sure, in the beginning of her marriage to Charley, she had been sure he would always love and cherish her. But that had been so long ago. She was another person now. A smarter person. And Nate was certainly not anything like Charley. She knew that with her mind. But something inside her obviously didn't believe it.

Charley had been her fairy-tale prince, and she'd loved him madly—until she realized he was really her worst nightmare.

Nate was the opposite of Charley. She didn't feel madly in love with him. Instead, she admired and respected his character and his actions. He made her laugh and encouraged her to do her best. Wasn't that love? The kind of love that was durable and liveable and happy-making. Nate was the real prince in her life.

Maybe that was her problem. For sure, she wasn't any man's princess. If Nate knew what she'd done... Just the thought made her shiver.

How could she be secure? Nate saw everything that was good about her, but he was blinded to her bad qualities. He thought she was a wise and good woman, and she wasn't either of those things. If he knew the truth about her—if he opened up his eyes and figured it out—he might turn from her. He might meet someone else. Someone who deserved him.

And if that happened, in her indignation and anger, she might do something that she could never forgive herself for doing.

She might kill him.

Seven

JULIAN AND AVERY sat on the stools by the bar, out of earshot from the other couple who'd slid into a booth, their arms on the wooden table, leaning toward each other. Two people having an intense discussion in the town's local pub.

"Where you from?" the bartender asked, a stocky man with a mustache and receding brown hair.

"Chicago," Julian said. "We love it there, but sometimes it's nice to get out of the big city."

"I bet. The wife and I and the kid went there a few years ago with friends and their kids. The guys got stuck going to the Museum of Science and Industry with the kids while the women shopped. I don't know how we got the raw end of the deal."

"You still whining about that?" A heavyset woman a few stools away plonked an elbow down on the bar top. "Troy's in high school now. That must've been ten years ago." She poked her index finger at the bartender. "And I bet you loved every minute in the museum."

The bartender smiled sheepishly. "It wasn't too

bad. They had lots of good things in there. But, man, was it crowded. I was glad to come home."

There was a mutter of agreement from the place that was about half full. Not a bad crowd for dinner time on Christmas Eve. Julian suspected this was the town watering hole where the natives gathered and gossiped and drank until at least half of them staggered outside.

"It's pretty here," Avery said. "Even with snow. Much prettier than Chicago. The snow is real white instead of dirty white."

"The minute you walked in," a male voice called out from a table behind them, "the place got even prettier."

Avery turned and giggled, her eyes bright. Julian turned, too. The guy laughing at her looked barely twenty. Leaning back on the wooden chair with his long legs spread open, Julian guessed he'd been the high school heartthrob.

Too bad for you. You'll never get Avery. I own her.

Julian grinned at the fool, as if he had no troubles. And he didn't have any. He just gave other people troubles.

The thought made him grin wider.

People as gullible as these didn't deserve to live.

An hour later, Julian and Avery left at the same time as the other bed-and-breakfast couple, who'd been talking intensely in the corner booth. No one said much during their walk, but the other couple held hands and shared meaningful gazes, and he was pretty sure they couldn't wait to get to their room and jump into bed. But when they stepped into the living room, Avery asked if they'd like to play a board game. The couple gazed at each other for a long moment, as if they were speaking telepathically. Then the wife nodded, and the man turned to them and agreed.

They played a game, and the other couple trounced them, the husband losing his cool and becoming aggressive. Good. That's what Julian liked. Opposition that would challenge him. Because so far it had been too damn easy.

The other couple won a second game, and Julian's muscles tightened around his shoulder blades to the point where it hurt. Despite the discomfort, he kept his smile. He wasn't going to let anyone see him as weak. And, really, he appreciated a war of intelligence. Because wasn't every game a war? One person won. One person lost.

This game was just pretend, but in the end, he would be the winner. And the others...well, they would be dead.

A streak of orange and white whipped out from behind the couch, racing to the kitchen. The girls gasped and then laughed.

The cat must have been scared and hiding. Smart animal. With maneuvers like that, when Julian and Avery left, there would be one living creature in the place. And if no one checked on Sylvia and her male guest for a few days, the cat would have the choice of four bodies to dine on.

Avery said something, and the other couple laughed. Julian smiled, the tension from losing easing away. Life was good. He was bad. That's the way he liked it.

And *this* was just the beginning...

After her months away from Trouble Bay, Sylvia felt constricted in her bedroom as she and Nate watched an old Susan Sarandon and Paul Newman movie on the sixteen-inch-flat screen TV on her dresser. Though cramped wasn't a bad thing when she was cuddled up against Nate, mulling over the options in her life.

Only one option stood out, but she needed to talk to Chuck before making any decisions. This was hard for her. Her late husband used to call her *rigid*—only he'd phrased it *stick up your butt*. At first she used to think that maybe she was at fault—

"What's wrong?"

She turned to look at Nate. "Bad memories."

He leaned over and kissed her cheek. Immediately, she felt better. Her mother used to kiss her on her cheek the few times when she'd done something exceptionally well. She'd been a good mother. Sylvia held nothing against her. But she'd been too busy to cuddle and kiss her only child often.

Sylvia had been a busy mom, too, but she'd made time for Chuck. He'd been an active and popular boy. She'd made special treats for him, she'd attended every school function, and she'd kept track of where he was. Not a helicopter parent, but she never forgot that there were often strangers in town. Strangers in their own house.

There had been a practical reason for her to have guns close by, in a place where only she had access to them.

Nate picked up the remote and muted the TV's volume. "Tell me about the bad memories."

She leaned her head on his shoulder again and watched the silent interaction of Susan and Paul. "My life is changing."

"How do you feel?"

"A little fearful."

He didn't say anything.

"Uncertain."

He still didn't say anything.

She looked at him. "Except for last year's break, I've been doing the same thing for more than thirty years. This is my home."

"You're a brave woman."

She thought of some of the things she'd done. She hadn't done them out of bravery but out of anger. That was...wrong. Soul-destroying. At a wedding reception years ago, she'd watched a small girl dancing with joy, and she'd decided to live with joy in her heart. She'd tried her best, but it wasn't easy to change. Since the wedding, she'd done a few things she wasn't proud of.

That needed to change.

"You can do anything you want," Nate said, as if he could hear the self-doubts and the self-recriminations that she couldn't seem to shake.

Maybe she wasn't meant to shake them. Not when she'd done something so serious. So final.

From the living room, she could hear the four

guests talking. And then there was a new sound, a small animal running in the hallway.

"The cat." She sat up and shoved aside the covers.

"You think you can catch it?"

She pushed out of bed, the carpet keeping her bare feet from getting too cold. "Maybe not, but at least she'll hear my voice. I want her to get used to me." She grabbed her robe from the chair in the corner. "I should go online and look up ways to lure a cat."

"I can tell you the answer," Nate said. "Food."

"I *am* feeding her." She heard the indignation in her voice. Taking care of unexpected guests was what she'd done for many years. The cat was like another guest, just more timid than most. "She's eating the food I put out for her."

"What? An eighth of a cup?"

"A *quarter* of a cup. And she's not full-grown yet." She put her hands on her hips. "She's the size of a squirrel, not a linebacker."

"How do you know it's a *she*?"

"The first time she jumped away from me, she exposed her belly and lower parts. There were no male parts sticking out. And what are you? A cat expert?"

"Not an expert, but real food is always better than canned."

"What do you suggest I feed her?" she asked. "A cow?"

"Honey, you don't have to be defensive. Do you have canned salmon? Cats like fish."

"I gave her tuna already." Sylvia narrowed her eyes. "I think you want to keep this cat."

"There's only one female in this house that I want to keep."

Her cheeks warmed, and she looked away, then back at him. "I'm not going anywhere."

"Neither am I, babe."

She sucked in her breath, feeling warm. She'd known this conversation was coming, but she wasn't ready for it. Not now.

"We're having turkey tomorrow," she said. "Chuck and Raine left one in the fridge. They even bought all the ingredients for the meal. I'll put half the leftover turkey in the freezer for them. We can take the other half back to Madison."

"If the cat leaves anything," he said. "It's my guess that she won't mind devouring the turkey leftovers."

Another thought popped up in her mind, and she frowned. Some days it seemed like there was always something new to worry about. Her motto should be, *I worry, thus I am.* "Will it bother you to celebrate Christmas with me?"

"You celebrated Chanukah with me already."

"I had a great dinner with your friends. Maureen is an amazing cook."

"*Our* friends," he said. "And how can I have a problem sharing your Christmas? I know it's supposed to be a celebration of Jesus's birth, but for me, it's a celebration of generosity, love, and good food. And I bet if Jesus is watching Earth from some heavenly place, he'll be nodding and smiling."

"And happy," she added, hearing the catch in her voice.

He nodded.

Her throat compressed with emotion. She bent down to kiss him, her hands on either side of his face. Just as he opened his mouth, she pulled back, laughing and flushed. They'd already made love, but the way she felt now was different. Too different, her chest too full of emotion to make sense of it right now.

"I have to go."

He caught her hand. "Now? You can't wait?"

"My mind is set. I need to catch a cat."

"How are you going to do that?"

"We have more tuna in the pantry, but we have canned chicken, too. I could try that."

"I always knew you were a smart lady."

"Really? Here I thought you just loved my body."

He laughed. A dirty, gritty, sexy laugh. She put on her slippers, then sashayed out of the room, making sure she gave Nate some hip movement to watch.

She wouldn't have to wait for Christmas for her joy. Right now, joy was inside her doing a happy dance.

Though she missed Chuck and Raine, she thought that this might be the best Christmas of her life.

To pull that off, she didn't need magic or even Santa Claus. All she had to do was stop worrying over something she'd done more than two decades ago.

In other words, she needed a Christmas miracle.

Eight

JULIAN'S ENERGY WAS high. He woke up with his body heated and a hard-on. Next to him, Avery snored softly, and he considered waking her. But not yet. He was too revved up, and his lovemaking would be too loud. Too feral.

Sometimes he liked to bite.

Sometimes she liked his teeth sinking into her flesh. Blood spurting out. He would lick it. Suck it in his mouth. The taste coppery on his tongue.

Sometimes he would be soft and gentle, and she would yell, "Harder! Harder! Hurt me!"

Sometimes he wouldn't hurt her. Just to torture her.

Sometimes he would. Hurting her until she screamed in pain. Screamed in ecstasy. Screamed his name.

He couldn't do that here. He couldn't take the chance that someone would hear her yell out his real name. Not with his next coup so close.

He slid out of bed, because if she woke up, she'd want more than he could give her right now. Barefooted, he strode to the bathroom, turning on the light when the door was nearly closed. Still not taking the chance of waking her.

Then he stood over the toilet and masturbated, imagining the other two women in the bed-and-breakfast. Both women were beautiful in their own way. One older and one younger. He would fuck them and fuck them and fuck them. He'd keep their men alive so they could watch. So they could hear the women's screams as he hurt them. One by one.

He wondered who would break first—the older man or the younger? Who would rush at him, yelling, arms out to push him away?

And as that happened, Avery—his darling sharpshooter—would pull the trigger of her Smith & Wesson, giggling with each bullet that met its mark.

No one would hear them. They were too far from their neighbors, who would be stuffed from their dinner after celebrating Christmas with friends and family. He could tell from their drive into Trouble Bay down Main Street, with every home decorated, that Trouble Bay was the kind of place that went all out for Christmas.

The perfect time to kill.

Grunting, he ejaculated, his breathing harsh and his legs weakened. Remaining standing, he gulped in air, his heart pounding.

After his heartbeat slowed and so did his breaths, he cleaned himself, then slipped back into the bedroom and the bed, his body relaxed.

He and Avery had come to Trouble Bay to see what they could get from the songwriter and her fiancé, who were also bed-and-breakfast hosts, according to the entertainment news. When he'd discovered the songwriter had left for the holidays, he hadn't wasted his time on anger. Instead, he'd thought of a way to salvage his trip here. A way they wouldn't come out of this empty-handed.

Sylvia looked like a woman who had money and jewels hidden away. Not flashy jewels but tasteful jewels. And Nate was the kind of ugly man women called cute. Cute because he had the buffoon smile, and he, too, looked like the kind of man who had money.

And if they didn't, well, he wasn't really doing this for the money. He was doing it because he could.

Maybe some other time, he would go after Sylvia's son and his songwriter girlfriend. It wasn't something he would obsess over. He didn't have obsessions. When you had obsessions, the obsession owned you.

Nothing owned him. Not even Avery.

As she would find out just before he killed her.

He would wait until she stopped being useful to him. It wouldn't take long to find a replacement. Perhaps the next time he'd choose a woman less eager to help him. A woman he would have to train to be compliant. A woman who would be so afraid of him she would never, ever do anything unless he snapped his fingers and allowed it.

In his bed again, he closed his eyes, his body calming as tendrils of sleep wrapped around him. Sometimes it almost seemed that what he did was too easy. People saw an attractive couple, and they immediately looked up to them and wanted to please them, even on their surly days.

It was true what the carnies said: *Everyone is a mark.* Only a few were the victimizer, the tormenter, the perpetrator.

The thief.

The murderer.

And politicians. In his opinion, some of the biggest thieves were politicians. Senators. Governors. Mayors.

Add bankers to the list. Drug companies. Doctors who were substituting *Give us more money* for *Do no harm.*

Maybe next time, he would strike one of the tricksters. Go for the higher stakes. They would have more money and possessions than a bed-and-breakfast owner.

Of course, where there was more money, there was more risk. And he wasn't in it for the money, though he liked the money just fine. Money was a bonus. It was power, and power was an aphrodisiac. As Lord Acton said in the early 1900s, "Absolute power corrupts absolutely."

He inhaled. Nothing wrong with that. Not when you were on the absolute power side of the fence. Nothing wrong at all.

Having lulled himself into a good mood, he closed his eyes, expecting to fall asleep soon. He always did. And usually with a smile.

Nine

"IT'S SNOWING OUT," Nate said.

Curled on her side of the bed, not fully awake yet, Sylvia squinted at Nate in his soft flannel pajamas. He was holding the curtain open, the weak rays of the morning sun peeking into the bedroom.

"Did I oversleep? What time is it?" She pushed up from the pillow. Normally an early riser, she'd had a hard time falling asleep last night. Change and a bad conscience were the culprits that had kept her awake.

He dropped the curtain and looked at the clock on the dresser. "Twenty to eight. You have plenty of time."

As she stumbled off to the bathroom, he added, "But don't count on the guests going to the resort for Christmas dinner."

She slowed and looked behind her.

"Remember the meteorologist last night forecasting two to three inches of snow?"

She didn't reply, but there was a bad feeling in her belly.

"He joked that it if the wind blew a few inches

the wrong way," Nate said, "the forecast could turn into a few feet."

The bad feeling in Sylvia's belly tightened.

"Guess what?" he asked.

"No guessing games. Just tell me."

He looked out the window again. "It's coming down pretty steadily. I'm not a meteorologist, but it's my guess that the wind is blowing the wrong way."

She headed to the bathroom. The snow could wait. Apparently it wasn't going anywhere.

And maybe Nate was wrong. After all, he hadn't won one lottery yet with his lucky numbers. Why should this be any different?

It was different. Upon returning from the bathroom, Sylvia's sweet and funny—and sometimes too annoyingly cheerful—boyfriend seemed fiendishly happy to tell her that the snow had gone off course.

"Sounds like my life," she said.

He smiled, his eyes warm. It took a lot to chip away his equanimity. "Since you've come into my life, every day has been better."

The coldness inside her that was saying this was the start of something bad melted like butter in the summer sun. She held out her arms to him, and they stepped toward each other. His arms around her, he kissed her.

"You're my woman, right?"

"You're crazy." She shook her head at him, but she was grinning as she stepped out of his hold.

"I need to get dressed and start breakfast. If it's still snowing, that's okay. Chuck and Raine decorated the tree in the front room, so that's done. And they did a great job of shopping for all the ingredients we'd need. Even the sweet potatoes. That was so nice of them."

"You did email them a list."

She made a face. "Am I too overbearing?"

"You know what you want. Nothing wrong with that. I'll thank Chuck for being so helpful."

She snorted a laugh. "Chuck and my soon-to-be daughter-in-law." She wanted to thank Raine for more than that. Mostly for making Chuck so happy and confident. At Chuck's core, he was the same man as before he'd met Raine, but now there was something extra. As if he'd stepped into his potential. It had been there all along, but having the right person to believe in him had pushed him to trample over the obstacles and go for the prize.

Like Nate believed in her. Her heart beat fast, but she turned away. Right now she didn't need a prize; she needed a shower.

"We just need dessert," Nate said in the kitchen twenty minutes later.

Sylvia laughed even as she shook her head. She and Nate had made a pact to stick to one sweet a day. She was doing well, but she wasn't sure about Nate. Other women smelled perfume on their man. She smelled chocolate.

"You decide on the dessert," she said, because

this was Christmas. And part of Christmas was stuffing yourself with too much food. Even desserts.

"Traditional," Nate said, without pause, as if this was something he'd been mulling over since she'd left the bedroom. "Apple pie or pumpkin."

"Either one is fine. We have a can of pumpkin pie filling in the cupboard and a bag of Granny Smith apples in the fridge. Whatever you decide, we should bake it this morning so we can have plenty of time to bake the turkey." She peered out the window. The snow looked to be blowing harder. She sighed. "Maybe it will stop soon and the guests can drive to the resort for dinner."

He was smiling as she turned back to him. No matter what happened, she knew he would enjoy it. He was like that.

She was a lucky woman. He was funny, sweet, and thoughtful. And a great lover. Maybe he looked like a slightly overweight Jewish comedian, but in bed he was, well, the best she'd ever had.

If there was a God, He—or *She*—possessed a peculiar sense of humor.

With a frown, she headed to the refrigerator. She had an omelet to make, and she didn't even know where this constant guilt was coming from lately. Maybe because she was feeling so lucky. Actually happy.

And deep down inside her, she knew she wasn't good enough for Nate.

Damn it, she'd *saved* people. And if she'd killed a murderer and a thief while doing so, then she should be lauded for it.

As for Charley...well, she didn't want to think about what had happened any longer. Enough about Charley. Enough.

She sucked in her breath and set the eggs on the counter, then reached for the bowl.

It slipped out of her grip, toppling to the floor. Shattering.

She put her hands on the sides of her cheeks. A sad, hurting moan came out of her mouth as Nate stepped over to put his arms around her, tugging her to his chest.

"It's okay," he said. "It's just a bowl. Nothing serious."

She moaned into the side of his neck.

"Are you all right? Did you hurt yourself?"

Tears were trailing down her face, and she couldn't pull away.

"What's the matter, baby?" he asked.

She shook her head.

"Are you sick?"

She shook her head again. She was always the strong one. Now she was turning to mush.

Consciences were a bitch.

He turned toward the closet where she kept the broom and dustpan. She should be doing that. Instead, she remained standing still, feeling stunned.

She knew what was wrong with her. She wanted to tell him the truth. Tell him what she'd done in the past. But she couldn't. She was confident that he wouldn't call the police, but how would he feel about living with a woman who'd killed her husband? He'd always wonder if he'd be next on the chopping block.

When he returned to sweep up the broken bowl into the dustpan, she still couldn't say anything. As if her voice were frozen, she watched him dump the shattered pieces into the garbage bag, then return the broom and dustpan to the closet.

"You're still crying," he said, his voice so tender, her heart ached.

As she shook her head, footsteps sounded from the hallway. She turned back to the counter and grabbed a napkin to wipe the tears from her face, then blew her nose in it.

She turned as Nolan and Erica, the dark-haired couple from the third floor, stepped into the kitchen. Erica, with her sleek, pulled-back hair and slender body and dark brown eyes that bored into Sylvia's, reminded Sylvia of the woman she'd shot a year and a half ago.

An icy chill shivered through her. Maybe that was the reason for all this guilt. Though she hadn't noticed the resemblance before now, her subconscious must have noticed it.

"Are you all right?" Erica's forehead puckered.

"I'm fine." Sylvia dredged up a smile. "Thank you for asking. Was there something you wanted?"

A blast of wind shook the house, and Sylvia shuddered.

"The Wi-Fi connection doesn't seem to be working," Erica said. "Neither does my phone's network. Does that happen often?"

Pulling on her outer mask of the perfect host, Sylvia turned to Nate. "Would you check the—" She stopped talking as Nate strode to the laptop on the counter.

Five seconds later, his mouth twisted ruefully and he shook his head. "Nothing."

"I hope it won't last long," Sylvia said as Nate got his phone out.

"Nothing here, either," he said.

"What do we do now?" Erica turned to Nolan.

"We'll eat breakfast. That will be done in about..." Nolan turned to Sylvia.

"Twenty minutes," she said.

Nolan turned back to Erica. "Twenty minutes."

Erica snapped around and stalked into the living room.

Nolan watched his wife, his body stiff.

Sylvia looked at Nate, but he just shook his head. She grimaced. This wasn't the first time she'd watched a marriage unravel in front of her eyes.

"There's a single-serve coffeemaker in the dining room," she said. "The coffee pods and a pitcher of water are on the buffet table. There's also hot water for tea and teabags."

Nolan nodded, but he continued to look after Erica, his facial muscles tightening and his eyes narrowing. His expression so fierce that Sylvia felt like an intruder watching him.

She didn't know why couples made each other unhappy, but it happened all the time, people walking around with open wounds that no doctor could heal.

Nolan stalked out of the kitchen. Sylvia let her breath out in a whoosh.

"You okay?" Nate asked.

"I've made a decision. If Chuck's business goes well this summer—and I have complete faith that it will—and if he agrees, I'm going to sell the bed-and-breakfast."

"And marry me?"

She swallowed, unable to look at his face.

"What's wrong?"

She shook her head. How could she tell him that she felt as if she'd been mooching off of him for the last year? He'd paid for almost everything, even the groceries. As a college professor and a mildly successful screenwriter with four screenplays sold, he wasn't poor, but he wasn't wealthy, either.

"I can see you thinking extra hard," he said.

"Is that a line from one of your screenplays?"

"Not yet." His eyes lit with humor. "But now that you've pointed it out, I might put it in my next one."

"I'm always thinking. Let's talk about this later."

He stepped closer to her. "Tell me one thing. Just start there. One thing, and I won't ask anything else until this evening."

"Not this evening," she said. "Tomorrow."

His face lit with laughter, and she snorted through her nose. Her nerves relaxed. She didn't know how, without saying one word, he could make her feel as if everything was going to be okay, but he did.

"Rock, paper, scissors?" he said.

Instead of replying, she put her hands on his shoulders, leaned forward, kissed him hard and fast, then stepped back. "I'll tell you one thing right now." Even as she said it, she felt the words in the back of her throat, ready to pour out as he looked at her with so much love in his eyes that it made her want to melt.

"Tell me," he said, his gaze still not leaving hers.

"In the beginning, I wasn't sure how long this would last. I just wanted..." She took a deep breath, and she shook her head, remembering her last Christmas. Calling him *her man.* Wanting him.

"Wanted what?" he asked.

"To be with a man who was smart and funny and lovable."

His eyes smiled at her, his cheeks pouching up. "That was my evil plan. From the first time I saw you, I was doing everything I could to convince you to live with me."

Despite the fear and the doubts inside her, like a merry-go-round she couldn't stop, she laughed. "You're not playing fair. You know I can't resist you when you make me laugh."

"There's no fairness in love." His smile was crooked, and his thick eyebrows hitched up. "I'm pulling out all the stops, baby."

She laughed again, shakily, tears close behind. "I can't tell you anything if I'm laughing too hard."

The humor remained in his face and his eyes, but he nodded. "In that case, no more funny business. Go on."

She took a deep breath. "I've always been independent. And you *are* my man."

"I am."

"But I need to do something productive. While Chuck is in charge, I'm not taking any money from him for the B and B. A few years ago, I had some house repair problems, mainly due to a local business owner in collusion with a crooked insurance agent—"

"Did you call the sheriff? A lawyer?"

"It's done. Over. I'm not looking backward; I'm going forward. And I can't go forward when I feel like a kept woman."

The skin around his eyes crinkled with laughter. "A *kept* woman?"

She fought back an urge to hit him. She knew what people saw when they looked at her. A fit blond woman who held her head high and walked with dignity with a slight smile on her face. A modern-day Grace Kelly, she'd been called by admirers in the past. She was sure she'd been called less flattering names, too, though not to her face.

Snobbish.

A woman who wouldn't get her hands dirty.

A woman who always did the right thing.

People who thought that had never seen her at a shooting range. Had never seen her painting bedrooms, cleaning toilets, and doing everything she could to save money.

"I'm not a wealthy man," Nate said, "but I'm not poor, either. I can take care of both of us. And if anything happens to me, I'll make sure you'll be taken care of. I love you, Sylvia." He took a step closer to her, until he was a hand-span away. "I'm pretty sure that you love me, too."

Tears warmed her eyes, and she wasn't the weepy type. She was the *grit your teeth and keep smiling until it's over* type. But now she stared at this man who made her laugh and feel taken care of, and she wanted to shout *Yes. Yes, yes, yes!*

But the last time she'd said yes to a man had ended up a disaster. The only wonderful thing that had come out of it was her son...and the revelation that she didn't need a man.

"Love isn't the point." She straightened her shoulders. "I'm *not* going to sponge off of you. I'll have some money. Chuck will be busy this spring and summer. The last time we spoke, he said that when he returned, he needed to talk to me. I'm pretty sure it's about the bed-and-breakfast. Last summer, his Trouble Bay Art Mart was a great success." She stopped and laughed shakily. "Okay, not a *great* success yet, but a *good* one. Enough so that even the most snobbish artists in the area who doubted him last year are asking him to include their artwork next year. It's just going to get bigger and better."

"Chuck had a great idea there." Nate reached up and caressed the side of her head. "He takes after his mother."

His words warmed her as she sniffed. "He's much better than his mother. He's..." She inhaled a deep breath. "He has a better heart than me. He thinks everyone is his friend. I make my friends prove their worthiness."

"Even me?"

"You're the exception. From the first time I met you in the grocery store, I liked you. You made me laugh."

"What I think," he said slowly, "is that you always feel the need to prove yourself."

She stared at him, her mouth open like a gaping fish before she closed it and shook her head. "I'm not making any final decisions until I talk to Chuck. If he agrees, I'll split the profits with him. I know he might not need the money now, but this place has been in our family for a long time. It's his as much as it's mine."

"Whatever you decide, it's your choice."

"I don't know what else I'll do, but I can't sponge off of you. I'll need to do *something*."

"You make great pies."

"So do many other people, and it's not what I want to do for a living."

"What are you good at?"

"That's the thing..." She took a deep breath. "You know that I've taken a few of our women friends in Madison to a shooting range and shown them how to shoot guns."

His eyes lit with humor. "You're thinking of giving target lessons to women?"

"Not quite that." She took a deep breath. "I'm thinking of opening up my own shooting range. Maybe I could have some self-protection classes, too." She shrugged. "It's just something I've been thinking about."

"Keep thinking." He patted her shoulder. "Quite a few women we know might be interested. Men, too. I'd go for the classes. Maybe you can work out special deals for students or groups of women."

Before she could reply, he turned and strode toward the living room. She watched him until a sound from the cloakroom made her turn her head.

The cat.

She shook her head. She had things to do. Feed the cat. Feed the guests.

Learn how to trust her heart.

Learn how to forgive herself.

Learn how to accept happiness.

She took a deep breath. For two decades, she'd been trying to do all three things. She was better now; if she weren't, she wouldn't have attracted her funny and smart professor. But forgiving herself wasn't easy.

Maybe because every once in a while she still had an urge to get out her gun and shoot someone.

Ten

"WE'RE REALLY GOING to shovel the neighbor's sidewalk?" Avery asked. Snow was pelting down, but she was bundled up in her winter coat, plus she wore a scarf and knitted hat that Sylvia had loaned her. She looked like she should be on a Christmas card, but first she'd have to stop scowling.

"Brownie points," Julian said. "Once the massacre is over, who will believe that we did the killing? We're the couple who crossed the street to shovel the sidewalk for the old lady at the deli. Everyone will be sure the killers were the other couple."

Avery leaned on her shovel, her back to the freezing wind. "When they find them dead and we're alive, that theory won't hold water."

A car was driving slowly down the icy street. "Who said they'll find them alive or dead?" he asked.

"You're not taking them with us."

He didn't answer. He just grinned.

Her mouth tightened. "It's the woman, isn't it? You think she's pretty, don't you?"

"If I do? What are you going to do about it?"

She glared at him. "One of these days, I'm going to kill you."

"You think so?" He smiled at her, his nerve endings revved up. All his senses on alert. This was what he loved about Avery. She could give almost as good as she got.

But not quite. He was the master; she was the apprentice. The master always won.

He pulled her to him and kissed her hard, grinding his teeth and his mouth against hers. He knew it hurt her, because it was uncomfortable to him.

Soft almost-cries came from her mouth beneath his, and he released her so fast she stumbled back a few steps, her breathing hoarse, her eyes on him, watching him the way she would watch a feral animal.

They stared at each other, then he nodded. "Let's shovel."

"Yes," she said. "Shovel." But she didn't move right away. She waited for him to turn away first.

As he shoveled, he listened. There was always the chance that she would lift up her shovel and slam it down on his head. He was ninety percent sure she wouldn't do it, but the thought kept him alert.

Because if anyone was going to be hurt, it wasn't going to be him. Not since he was an adult.

As a child, he'd learned an important lesson. There's always one who hurts...and there's also one who gets hurt.

He preferred to be the one who did the hurting.

A soft laugh came out of his mouth, then he began to hum the Merry Christmas song. Why not? Everything was coming together. He'd been getting blasé about the killings. In the beginning, they'd excited him, but the last couple had been...bland. Ordinary. Anyone could have planned them. Anyone could have done them. He'd even found an online page that showed a blurred image of him and Avery—not as they looked now, of course—with people talking about how they'd do it better.

At first, it had amused him. Then it had infuriated him. And people called *him* sick.

Now he was happy again. He hadn't been this excited in a long time.

"You know what?" he asked Avery.

She looked at him warily. She could read him better than anyone, and she must have realized she'd gone too far. "What?"

"Christmas really is the best time of the year." He turned and started shoveling, singing softly, "Jingle bells, jingle bells, jingle all the way..."

As he sang, he thought that anything could be a weapon. Even a shovel.

Or a branch from a fake Christmas tree. Just pull it out and stick the thick wire end into someone's neck.

Yes. Anything could make a good weapon. All you needed was opportunity and luck.

Footsteps stomped on the bed-and-breakfast driveway. Julian changed the angle of his shoveling in time to see the two other guests stomping across, the man first. They stepped inside, but in less than a minute, they were walking out the garage's side door. They each carried a shovel as they headed down the driveway and—if he wasn't wrong—straight toward him and Avery.

Well, well, well. Here was opportunity and luck coming straight toward him. The time wasn't right to take advantage of it yet, but he'd grab that advantage with both hands soon. And once he grabbed it, there would be blood.

A pumpkin pie and an apple pie sat on the counter. Sylvia had made the stuffing with Nate's help. He wasn't a brilliant chef, but he was an intelligent man, capable of cutting up celery and onions without slicing a finger open. It seemed like something that almost every able-bodied adult person could do, but she'd discovered that some men fumbled the job on purpose or thought that cutting fruits and vegetables was beneath their manly skills.

Once again, she pictured Charley, her late-and-unlamented husband. She quickly shut down those thoughts, angry at herself. She was so tired of thinking about him.

Good things were happening in her life, and it was time for her to think forward instead of backward. Time to focus on the good.

She shifted her thoughts to the turkey as she washed her hands in the sink. She'd put it in the oven just before noon. Plenty of time for it to roast before dinner tonight. She had stuffing in the cavity, and some leftover dressing was in a bowl on the counter.

Her kitchen smelled wonderful.

Even the cat thought so. Sylvia had spotted the cat sneaking in, then running back to the cloakroom whenever she felt Sylvia's gaze on her.

It was time to fix that.

She opened a can of wild-caught crab meat. Raine, Chuck's triple-Grammy-winning fiancée, had expensive tastes, but she could afford them. From the bottom of the cupboard, in a hard-to-reach place, Sylvia took out another small china plate, this one with a rose design, and used her fingers to pull out a tablespoon of crab for the cat.

Her fingers smelled of crab now, but she decided not to wash them yet. She might be on to something. *Canned crab. The perfect perfume for cat lovers.*

Inside the cloakroom a moment later, she peered downward and around, the plate in her hand. As soon as she spotted four small legs and paws in the farthest corner, she turned the closet light on and closed the door. Only then did set the plate down.

She stepped to the other side of the closet and sat down. Crossing her legs, she waited for the cat to get hungry enough to steal out of her hiding place. She didn't know why she was putting herself through so much trouble for a cat that she wouldn't be keeping. She wasn't known as softhearted. But the cat was so afraid and so skinny—on the edge of starvation—that it touched even her reluctant heart.

Twenty minutes later, the cloakroom door opened. The cat stopped licking Sylvia's fingers, then she squawked and leapt away, hiding behind a pair of Chuck's boots in the corner.

Sylvia sighed and peered up at Nate. "Bad timing. She just got up enough courage to lick my finger."

"I knew you could charm me, but I didn't know you were a cat whisperer, too."

"I used my secret power." She wiggled the fingers of her right hand. "*Eau de* crab."

He chuckled. "You're going to a lot of effort for the cat."

"Not really." She pushed up to her feet, then brushed off her butt, which was cold now. If she did this again, she would bring a towel to sit on. "It's Christmas. A good time to make someone else happy. I've never had a cat before."

"I've had a couple over the years. I like dogs, too, but they're more dependent than cats, and I'm a selfish man."

"You're the most generous man I know." She bent to pick up the empty plate.

"To you, I am."

"And your students."

"It strokes my ego to help them."

She narrowed her eyes at him.

"You're giving me the stink eye," he said.

"I do that when a man lies to me." She took a breath. "Or lies to himself."

"If I help my students, they're grateful to me. Gratitude is a real ego boost. Some people get off on being powerful. Others get off on being helpful." He wiggled his eyebrows. "Or making love to a beautiful woman."

She laughed. "Don't change the subject. When one of your students is successful, you're as thrilled as they are."

"And when I'm making love to that beautiful woman?" His brown eyes seemed darker in the cloakroom with the small light.

"Okay, I give up." She threw up her hands. "You are the most wonderful man I know. Why haven't you married before?"

There was a stillness behind her as she stood. She felt the tension in her chest, and she slowly turned to look at him. His normally cheerful expression was sad.

"You've never asked about my past," he said.

"I've always thought you lived in the present. You told me about your parents and your sister." His sister lived in Paris with her doctor husband, and she had two sons. His parents had passed before she'd met him.

"You never asked why I never married."

"I wondered." Her heart beat a little faster.

"Because I'm such a catch," he said, a small twinkle back in his eyes.

A shudder of relief shivered through her, and she took a deep breath. "You're making a joke, but I think you are a catch. Do you want to tell me about it?"

"I made a promise not to tell anyone."

"In that case—" She stepped forward, expecting him to move back.

He didn't move, standing solidly in the cloakroom doorway. "I'm breaking that promise. I have to. I want to marry you, Sylvia, and you deserve to know my past."

Her muscles tensed. If he told her his past, he would expect her to tell him hers. But she had secrets she could never tell. Not when these words were blisters in her belly.

"I was in love." His voice was slow. Hushed. "She died four years ago. We were lovers for twenty years. She was married, and in her own way, she admired her husband and didn't want to divorce him."

"He was wealthy, right?"

"That wasn't it. She didn't want to hurt him."

"Really? So instead of hurting him, she cheated with you for twenty years?" Her voice rose with every word. "And you didn't quite answer me. Was her husband wealthy or not?"

He set his lips together.

She nodded sharply. "That's what I thought."

A meow came from the back of the cloakroom as she marched past Nate.

He followed her. "I did try to break it off. I dated other women, but she needed me. She was going through some bad times."

In the kitchen, she whirled to face him. "That's too bad. If the times were so bad, she should have left him. As someone who was cheated on, I don't have a lot of respect for cheaters. Is that why you didn't tell me?" She poked her finger in the air at him, and his eyes widened in surprise, then narrowed.

He didn't appreciate her reaction. Too bad. This was what an angry woman looked like. "Your girlfriend wanted it all. She wanted you with your wit and your love. Your adoration. And she wanted her wealthy husband with all the privilege and status that went with it. I have no respect for her. And I'm kind of losing respect for you."

She whirled around again.

He clasped his hand around her upper arm. "Are you jealous?"

"Of a dead woman? No."

He stepped in front of her. "What are you thinking?"

"You don't want to know what I'm thinking." She sucked in a breath. She wasn't about to share her mixed feelings. And it didn't matter that none of this made sense. She didn't know his former lover. Maybe she'd been a saint. And who was she to judge? What she'd done in her life was so much worse than what he'd done.

That knowledge didn't change anything. She was furious anyway.

And at least she wasn't thinking of getting out her gun.

"You're angry."

"Bingo. I'm angry, and you're brilliant."

"I am sorry."

"Sorry I found out." She crossed her arms. "Sorry you told me."

"Sorry I did it. But there's something more."

She stared at him. Not saying anything.

Neither did he, his lips working but nothing coming out of his mouth.

It must be important. It must be... She hissed in her breath. "A child? Did you and she have a child?"

"How did you..." He shook his head. "Hayley's twenty-two. She doesn't know she's my daughter. She's in London now, going to Oxford. She calls me Uncle Nate. We text jokes a few times a week." As he spoke, his cheeks and nose reddened. "I had to be a friend of the family. It was the only way I could keep in touch with her."

Sylvia sighed, her anger melted. Nate was miserable about this. Unhappy. He needed her.

Putting her arms out, she stepped up to him and hugged him tightly. He hugged her back harder, his heart pounding against her chest.

Later, they would talk about this. His daughter needed to know the truth about him. Know who her real father was.

But not now. Now he didn't need advice. In fact, he didn't *want* her advice. He didn't want a lecture. He wanted comfort.

That's what she would give him.

The back door opened. Voices came from the back hall. Their guests. They'd volunteered to shovel the front sidewalk for the deli and the bed-and-breakfast in return for the dinner, though she hadn't asked them to do anything. After all, it was Christmas, and it was snowing out. She wanted this to be a happy day for her guests. A happy time for her and Nate.

The two couples certainly sounded in a good mood, though their timing was lousy.

Nate stepped back just as there was a squeal from the hall. The next second the cat streaked out of the cloakroom, racing across the kitchen, into the living room.

Sylvia switched her gaze from the streaking tabby to Nate. Normally she'd expect him to chuckle at the cat's antics, but he shook his head.

"I have to go," he said, his voice hoarse, his eyes blinking. He headed down the hall to their bedroom.

Sylvia stared after him. She felt an intense desire to fall down on her knees and curl her hands into fists and pound the kitchen tile.

But that was too dramatic for her. Instead, she sucked in her breath, turned around, and forced her lips into a smile.

Right now, she'd be glad when this holiday was over, the guests were gone, and the cat...

No. Not the cat. If her life was changing, she was going to live it her way. And she just realized that maybe her way included a tiger-striped cat.

She wasn't ready to commit, but now it was her heart that was beating wildly.

Eleven

CAT BREATHED HARD behind the couch, shaking. There were too many humans in this house. She knew about humans. They yelled. They threw things. They smelled bad.

They were stepping into the room now.

Quivering harder, Cat crouched and waited for the humans to leave.

Two of the humans were males, and Cat didn't trust human males with hard voices. Or human females with sharp voices.

Cat waited for them to go away. But instead of going away, they sat down. Talking loudly and laughing. Especially the human males. Especially the one with the voice that said, *I'm smarter and stronger than you.* The voice of a leader. A voice that said he was the big dog, and he would hurt anyone who got in his way.

Sylvia made hot chocolate on the stove, then carried it into the living room. Nolan and Erica were sitting on the couch, holding hands. The stony expressions from yesterday were gone. Good. This might be her last time in charge of the B and B, and she wanted it to be a great experience for both couples.

"This is so sweet of you." Taylor smiled brilliantly.

"You're the best hostess ever." Brad grinned.

"It's no trouble," Sylvia said. She wished she were one of those gregarious people who could smile back and say something that would make everyone laugh. But she'd never been that way. She'd always been the one secretly finding fault, even if she did keep it to herself.

That was the old Sylvia. The new Sylvia had too many faults of her own to worry about other people's imperfections. Like Taylor and Brad's perpetual cuteness. As sickening to her as too much sugar in a dessert.

She turned to the other two. No cuteness here. Just...something dark and serious, though she didn't know what. But as she looked into Nolan's dark eyes, she had an uneasy feeling that he was hiding something.

"Nolan and I will share this." Erica grabbed one mug, then glanced at Nolan with apprehension. His lips pinched together, and he nodded slightly.

Goose bumps crawled down Sylvia's spine.

She turned away. Whatever was happening with the couple was none of her business. "Dinner will be ready at five. If you'd like a snack before then, the diner across the street is open until two."

"I saw that when we were shoveling." Brad's

eyebrows rose. "Who goes there in this weather?"

"Locals, especially this time of year. A short walk for most of us." Sylvia shrugged. "We're hardy people in Trouble Bay."

Taylor shuddered. "Hardier than I am."

"You just shoveled," Sylvia smiled at her. "You're hardier than you think."

"Your kitchen smells heavenly." Erica glanced at Nolan again. "But I'm not that hungry. I can wait until dinner."

"I'll wait, too," Nolan said.

Sylvia nodded, keeping her expression neutral though all her instincts were on alert. "I can serve fruit, cheese, and crackers. Cookies, too, of course."

"That's too much trouble," Taylor said in her cheery voice. "It's nice enough for you to let us all join you and Nate for dinner."

"It's my pleasure. I want this to be a wonderful experience for all of you."

"It's the most wonderful time of the year." Brad beamed at her. "Already, I can tell it will be an experience that I'll never forget."

Taylor giggled and put her hand over her mouth. "Me, too."

Erica and Nolan looked at them without saying anything, their lips pressed together, then turned their somber gazes to Sylvia.

A chill shivered through Sylvia. A feeling that she needed to get away from these people.

Stepping back, she kept her polite smile on and told them the could use the coffee maker on the buffet in the dining room whenever they pleased. She didn't say it, but she decided to put fruit and cookies out for the guests, too. If she was going to do something, she wanted to do it right.

As she strode out of the living room, a noise slowed her. Something thumping after her, the sound like a herd of wildebeest, followed by a burst of laughter from her guests. The next instant a tiger-striped streak raced past her.

The cat.

Sylvia's shoulders relaxed. As if something wrong had been averted, and now it was okay again. She hurried into the kitchen after the cat. The cat was way ahead of her, racing through the kitchen, into the hallway, then zipping into the cloakroom. Sylvia stood still in the kitchen, imagining the cat shaking behind the couch the whole time she'd been hiding in the living room. Frightened. Feeling unsafe.

Probably no place had been safe for the cat since shortly after she'd been born, which was a sad, sad thing.

She should have put the litter box and the food in Chuck's bedroom, but if she transferred the litter box and the water and food bowls now, the cat would be confused. Besides, the two couples would be leaving tomorrow morning. She didn't expect any more guests, and it wasn't worth changing anything.

She set the tray on the counter, then turned toward the bedroom. This had been an unsettling day. Her anger at Nate was gone now. After all, his former lover had been a selfish bitch. So? That wasn't a mortal sin. And knowing Nate, not being able to claim his daughter must eat at him a little every day.

She stopped as she reached the closed bedroom door, then took a big breath and strode back to the kitchen, holding her head high.

Let him brood. Sometimes it felt to her as if everyone had their own hell to go through. Even the cat. No wonder she wanted to hug the cat. No wonder she put off calling the Humane Society right away. She and the cat had a lot in common.

Twelve

"CAN I HELP with anything?" Erica asked.

Sylvia started, then twisted around. She'd heard numerous footsteps finally going to the different floors about twenty minutes ago, but Erica must have remained downstairs. There was tension in Erica's face now, her eyes shadowed.

Unease spread inside Sylvia. She'd been right. Something was wrong with Erica and Nolan.

"Everything is almost done," Sylvia said. "I'm just about to make my garlic snap bean recipe."

"I *love* snap beans and garlic," Erica said with the fervor that most woman her age used to describe a boyfriend or a chocolate dessert. She immediately made a face. "That sounded weird, didn't it?"

"A little. But given what's going on in the world, I'd prefer to obsess over snap beans and garlic than, say, a thousand-dollar pair of shoes."

Erica giggled, then put her long fingers over her mouth, stopping the sound. As if humor wasn't something she should do.

Sylvia understood that, too. For too many

years, she had laughed guardedly. As if she didn't deserve to be happy. Not even for a moment.

"What kind of a snap bean dish do you make?" she asked. Better to stick to the subject of food. Food was safe.

"My favorite is with garlic, ginger, and sliced almonds. If you don't have—"

"That sounds wonderful, and I have all of that." Sylvia stepped back. "I'll get the ingredients, and you can put it together. What else do you need?"

Erica's eyes brightened, but as she rattled off a few more ingredients, Sylvia still felt a sense of wrongness. A bad vibration in the air that had nothing to do with the snow and a possible blizzard. Already the corners of Erica's mouth were curving down, her eyebrows contracting in distress.

Erica's husband, Nolan, was as intense as Erica, but in a different way. Every time Sylvia looked at him, she felt as if an invisible dark cloud hovered above his head.

Frowning, Sylvia stepped to the pantry to collect the ingredients. She wasn't a fanciful person. Her intuition was telling her something about Nolan, and she'd learned to listen to it.

She would keep her eyes and her mind open.

"Here you all are!" Taylor's cheerful voice vibrated in the kitchen.

Sylvia turned from the pantry, then set the bottles and herbs on the counter. Unless her guests misbehaved or broke something or left their rooms a mess, she had no opinion of them. But the snowstorm had changed everything, throwing them together for this short time. Whether they liked it or not.

For Sylvia, it was a big, fat *not* when it came to Taylor, though she had nothing against Taylor except her constant sunniness. Sylvia had just never been a fan of overly cheerful people. To her, Taylor's super-happy demeanor was just, well, irritating. It was a fault of hers, Sylvia knew, and someday she would be a grumpy old woman. If that was the case, then so be it.

She couldn't say she liked Erica, either, but she had nothing against her, and Erica's garlicky snap bean recipe did sound interesting. An Oriental touch to the American dinner, and Nate would like it, too.

"I didn't hear you," Sylvia said. "I thought you were upstairs."

"I'm wearing my suede boots." Taylor raised her right foot and wiggled it. "The soles are suede, too. They're comfy and warm."

"They look comfortable," Sylvia said. "Did you need anything?"

"I'm fine! I'm wonderful!"

Sylvia silently groaned. That was way too much enthusiasm.

"The Internet still isn't working," Taylor said.

"There are books in the living room," Sylvia said.

"Oh, I never read books."

Erica made a choking sound.

"You're getting everything ready," Taylor said. "This is so fun! All the ladies getting the food ready. What can I do?"

"Everything is done already except the beans."

Sylvia smiled politely. "It's Erica's recipe, and I'm not even doing anything with it. If you're looking for something to do, there are picture puzzles in the living room. Or you might like some of the magazines." She stopped herself from saying, *They have pictures.*

"I'm in your way, aren't I?" Taylor's lips pouted.

"If it's all right with you, Sylvia," Erica said, "Taylor can help me finish the snap beans. You've done so much already. You deserve a break."

"Yes." Taylor's face was bright again. "I'm actually very good in the kitchen."

Sylvia backed away, thanking both women. She was tired. Perhaps more emotionally tired than physically. And she'd been a little bitchy toward Taylor, not as gracious as she should be.

As she neared her bedroom, she wondered where all the men were. Probably watching football in their rooms.

She gripped the door handle, then turned it. Something made her look behind her, and she caught Taylor and Erica standing in the hallway by the kitchen, watching her.

Without a word, she turned to the door, opened it, stepped inside, and closed it softly. Then she did something she normally didn't do until she went to bed for the night when they had guests. She locked the door behind her.

The sound of snoring greeted her. Nate. On his back on the bed, the cover over him, his mouth open.

She sat on the chair in the corner and rocked back and forth, her hands over her mouth to silence her laughter that threatened to turn into hysteria.

After a moment, the urge to laugh stopped and her hands dropped to her lap. She remained in the chair and just sat, closing her eyes and clearing her mind. Concentrating on her breaths. A form of meditation that she had begun every morning during her last few months in Madison. Since she'd returned to Trouble Bay, she'd been pulled back into a different rhythm.

She inhaled deeply, then exhaled slowly. Going into the zone, ignoring the occasional drifting thought, even the one that reminded her of the sense of danger she'd felt. Then the next one that told her she should get her gun out. That she should be prepared.

That she should—

The bed creaked, startling her.

"Hello, darling," Nate said.

She opened her eyes. Nate was standing next to the bed wearing his jeans and a blue sweatshirt.

Her heart warmed. She had fond memories of a favorite teddy bear from when she was a child, until her mother had said she was too old for it and had thrown it in the trash. She'd cried for hours. Sorrowful, hiccupping sobs.

Now Nate was her living, breathing teddy bear.

Still in the calm meditation zone, she wasn't angry at her mother anymore. Instead she was grateful for Nate. Most women she knew drooled over lean and muscled men, but she preferred her human teddy bear any day.

Especially when he looked at her with warm eyes.

"I know what the answer is going to be," he said, "but do you need help in the kitchen?"

"Taylor and Erica are making the last dish. The turkey is in the oven. Everything else is done."

"Is there anything I can do for you?"

"Why, yes, there is." She grinned at him, feeling happy. Euphoric. Still partially in the meditation zone.

"And that *anything* is?" Nate grinned back at her.

"You're a smart man. I'll let you guess."

He laughed, his eyes bright, his smile wide. "I'll brush my teeth first."

As he left for the bathroom, she sat back. Relaxed now, she let her mind wander, her thoughts disjointed. Somewhere in her mind was the suggestion that she arm herself. She remained seated for a few long moments.

Finally, she stood—

Nate strode back into the bedroom, closing the door behind him, grinning, his eyes bright. "Ready?"

Not saying a word, she stepped toward him, her arms out, a tide of desire and happiness rising inside her.

Right now, this was all that mattered.

"I love you," he said.

"I love you, too." And it was true. The *you make me happy love*, which was much better than the *I don't want to live without you love*. And thank God for that.

Thirteen

AVERY DREW JULIAN into the cloakroom, the door open enough to let in light from the hallway. "Sylvia suspects something," she said, her voice low even though the others weren't around.

Julian gripped Avery's arms, and he felt the slight muscle beneath his fingers and the thin sweater that she wore. He squeezed the muscles, and she stared at him, breathing hard. Only when her breath slowed did he loosen his grip. Still holding her, but not as tightly.

"You're panicking," he said. "Why?"

"It felt like she was looking through me," she whispered. "Like she was suspicious."

"No one ever suspects you. Did you do anything? Say anything?"

"No! I was as nice as ever. I wasn't fawning over her, of course, but—"

"Of course not," he said, making his tone smooth.

And then he squeezed her biceps again. She sucked in her breath until he released her.

Now she would behave. Now she would

remember that she needed to be calm and in control, as he'd taught her.

"Did she say anything?"

She shook her head, not taking her eyes off of his face.

"Baby, are you losing your nerve?"

"No." She shook her head wildly. "Never."

"If you are, now is the time to tell me. Fear is death. Fear is being strangled." He stared into her widening eyes.

"I don't know what was wrong."

"Christmas," he said, his voice mocking. "The season of love. You come from a conventional family. Are you missing them?"

He pictured in his mind her parents lying on the floor in their suburban house. Their eyes open with shock and horror, even in death.

He'd killed them.

She'd killed her thirteen-year-old sister. Stabbed her sister in her belly and whispered just loud enough for him to hear, "You'll be better off dead."

He'd never asked her, but he'd suspected she'd done that to keep him from fucking her sister. And he would have. Afterward, he'd fucked Avery twice before they left in the middle of the night and drove to their apartment.

The thought made him want her. Right now. Right here. When he'd strode through the kitchen, Sylvia and Nate weren't around, but he'd heard muted voices from down the hallway in their private rooms. The other couple were in their suite now. He and Avery were the only ones in this area of the bed-and-breakfast. The snow was still coming down swiftly. There was plenty of food in the house, and no one was going outside.

The Internet was still down. As far as he knew, the other two couples were either sleeping or fucking right this minute.

He knew which one he wanted to do. He put his arms around her back. "I'm going to fuck you."

"Good." She started to turn toward the hall, and he held her back.

"Here."

Her eyes widened. "Someone will see us."

"Probably not." Every cell inside him felt alive. "And if they do, they'll be embarrassed, not us."

She giggled nervously, and he liked her nervousness. He liked keeping her on her toes. Gentle one time. Hard the next.

This time was not going to be gentle. Or pretty.

He was as aroused as a man could be. This was going to be fast and ugly. He clutched her shoulders, then he shoved her as hard as he could against the coats and jackets, pushing her to the cloakroom wall.

A shriek came. Loud and sharp. He dropped his hands. *What the—*

Something knocked into his right leg, just below his calf. He started to lose his balance, his arms flailing. Another high-pitched shriek hurt his ear. He glanced down and lost his balance again. Out of the corner of his eye, he saw a tiger-striped streak.

And then it was gone.

"Fuck," he said. "Fuck, fuck, fuck. What the fuck was that?"

"The cat." Her voice was shaky. "The one that Sylvia's planning on taking to the Humane Society when the holidays are over."

"That's one more thing she won't have to worry about. After tonight, neither she nor her chubby boyfriend will be breathing."

"And the cat?" Avery giggled nervously.

He grabbed her arm and pulled her out of the closet. The cat had been a reminder to him to keep on his toes. Their last few adventures had been easy, but he would not be complacent. He would not be foolish.

There was no way he would walk away from this place with nothing. With failure. He would not allow it.

"Didn't you hear the Christmas poem?" he asked. "*Not a creature was stirring, not even a mouse.* In this case, when we leave, it will be a cat."

Fourteen

THE CAT.

Nate and Sylvia were under the covers, next to each other, breathing heavily from their recent activity, when she heard pounding coming from the cloakroom, across the kitchen floor, and heading into the hallway.

She jumped off the bed, then hurried to open the door just far enough to stick her head into the hallway, her unclothed body getting chill bumps as the cat screeched and flew into the room. Not seeing anyone chasing the cat—for which she thanked God—she closed the door, then turned around in time to see the cat dive under the bed.

Nate pushed up on his elbows, looking bemused. "What was that?"

"The cat." Her heart thumping, Sylvia grabbed her cotton undies from the chair where her clothes were neatly folded, put them on, then her bra. "Something spooked her. It sounded like she was running for her life."

The sound of hurried footsteps came from the kitchen, and she stilled, listening as the footsteps headed to the living room, then to the stairway.

She looked up at the ceiling. As if she could see through it. She turned back to Nate.

"Sounds like two guests," Nate said.

She tugged her sweater over her head, pulling it down before she spoke. "Maybe they forgot something."

"Or maybe they thought it would be a fun place to have sex."

"My *kitchen*?" Her sentence ended with a squeak.

"The cloakroom is my guess. We should try it sometime." He grinned, sparks in his eyes. Like a small boy who'd just committed mischief in his classroom.

Shaking her head but laughing softly, she put on her thick cotton socks, then pulled on her pants. She knelt, her bottom in the air, and gazed under the bed. It was a dark place, and the mattress sagged slightly where Nate was lying. Once again she spotted the cat's green eyes first, the rest of her body blending in with the shadows.

"Hey, kitty," she said. "Are you all right? Did the man and woman scare you?"

The bed creaked, the springs and the mattress moving. The cat backed up toward the wall behind the headboard as Nate got out of bed. As Sylvia turned her head, she could see Nate's pale but shapely feet with hairs growing above his ankles.

She had an urge to wrap her hand around his ankle and kiss his calf. Then kiss him all the way up the insides of his legs.

The thought made her grin. Everyone thought she was so upright and stiff. But she could be spontaneous.

Not now, though. *Now* was all about the scared cat under her bed.

"Sweetheart," she said, looking back under the bed.

"I like your position," Nate said.

She raised her left arm behind her and showed him her middle finger.

He laughed.

"Here, kitty." Her chin touched the carpet. "You can come to me. I won't hurt you."

A minute passed as she heard Nate pulling on his clothes while she tried to coax the cat out. Finally, she pushed up and sat back on her calves, twisting to look at Nate, who was putting on his shoes now.

"The cloakroom wasn't a great idea," she said. "I should put her water and food dishes in a different room."

"One of the guest suites?"

"I can't do that. Those are our money rooms."

"No one is staying in them."

"She could have an accident. Or she might turn out to be one of those cats that has a urination problem."

"I suppose you want to name her."

She blinked. "What if I do?"

He stilled. "It's a commitment."

"You name her. You're the writer. You'll think of something worthy for her."

He laughed. "Oh no. Not me. Once you name an animal, it's yours."

She stared at him, not saying anything. "Or ours?"

He looked at her for a long moment, and

something changed in his face, his eyes glowing. "What are you saying?"

She felt a surge of emotion, but it wasn't happiness. It was fear.

"The cat's a bit of a fraidycat," he said slowly, but his gaze remained on her, "so I think she could use a strong name to grow into. I like Teela. It's from He-Man cartoons in the eighties. *The Masters of the Universe*. Her mother was a sorcerer, and Teela was a kickass warrior."

"I like that." She scrambled up and held out her arms, but everything felt wrong. As if she were a beat behind a refrain. As if she'd missed something important.

He stood, too, and they kissed each other. An after-sex kiss, but there was more to it. Almost a sense of desperation.

What there wasn't was words of love. Laughter. Bright smiles.

She pulled back. Something still felt wrong. As if they were afraid to say anything. As if their relationship was so fragile that one wrong word would break it, so it was better to not say anything.

And right now, Teela came first. She was a survivor. A frightened survivor. A little thing, with hardly any fat on her to insulate her from the below-zero nights. If they hadn't taken her in, Sylvia was sure she would have frozen to death.

"I'll put her water and food bowl in Chuck's room." Nate stepped toward the door. "What about the litter box?"

"Not Chuck's room. What if she has an accident in their room?"

He stopped. She could see the careful look on his face, the way he looked at her as if he wondered how to reply without saying, *What the hell happened to the smart woman I know?*

She could tell him that smart didn't mean she ignored her heart. Her heart was telling her that the cat needed her, but it still didn't change her fastidious nature.

"Besides," she said, "if we put Teela's food, water, and litter box in Chuck's bedroom, she might not come out. She needs to get used to people."

"You mean she needs to get used to you and me," he said. "What do you really want?"

She shook her head. She wanted...*everything.* "I'd like to keep her, but I'm not sure..." She took a deep breath. "Teela might be happier living with Chuck and Raine. I'm pretty sure that they won't want to keep the B and B going. They'll want their own place. Maybe they'll like Teela."

His smile was gone, his face serious. "In that case, it looks like we have a temporary roommate. I'll get her food, the water, and the litter box. If there's an accident, I'll clean it."

Sylvia watched him step into the hall, closing the door behind him. And she felt something else shut, too. A door in her heart, or maybe a window, which was ridiculous. That something she would read in a poem or a song. It wasn't real life. A real heart.

And she was pretty sure that if the cat had any toilet accidents, she would be the one cleaning it up long before Nate did. Not because he didn't mean it, but as Chuck liked to say, she was a clean freak. She shrugged. It wouldn't be the first time she'd cleaned up a mess. And it might not even happen.

She turned back to the bed, then got down on her knees again, peering below the mattress. "Hello, Teela. How do you like your name?"

No reply came, but the glowing green gaze never left her face.

"Why do I feel that you need me so badly?" Sylvia asked.

Teela meowed, and Sylvia felt a ball of warmth curl around her heart. "I'm going to make you love me," she whispered. Then she sat back and looked behind her, to make sure no one had sneaked behind her and was listening.

What the hell was she doing? Of course she wasn't going to make Teela love her, only to leave her, and it was a good thing that Teela didn't know what she was saying. She may have committed a few mortal sins, but she'd never broken anyone's heart.

Not even a cat's.

Fifteen

THE MAN LEFT, and only the woman stayed. She talked to Cat, her words falling lightly onto Cat's ears. The woman's voice was safe. Quiet but smooth. Not loud and angry. Not pitched too high and screechy, like an angry bird. The woman had a voice that could almost be a cat's voice.

It reminded Cat of the time when she was with her mom and her brother and her sisters.

Cat didn't know where the others were now. There was just her and the lady with the good voice that wasn't too soft or too hard. And the man, too. The man's voice wasn't soft, but neither was it angry. Cat could tolerate him. And he was gone now, in another part of the house. If he came back to this room, that would be all right with Cat, though she would be cautious of him.

If he never came back, that would be better.

The other people in the house didn't bother Cat—as long as they stayed away from her. If they came too close, she would run and hide.

Footsteps were plodding in the hallway, coming closer. By now, Cat knew the steps and the scents of all the different humans in the house, and these belonged to the man. He was coming back after all.

Cat smelled her box, the scent familiar, even before the man carried it into the room, then set it down in a corner farthest from the bed. The whole time he was in the room, Cat remained tense, ready to race away or to stay. The man stood by the door to the hallway, then turned to say something to the woman, his mouth open.

But no voice came out of his open mouth. Until finally, from deep in his throat, there came a gargling sound. As Cat scrambled back under the bed, the man turned again and left, closing the door behind him, but not all the way.

Still keeping an eye and an ear out for the man's return, Cat crept closer to the side of the bed where the woman sat.

"You're coming to me." The woman's voice lilted, sounding similar to Cat's purring voice.

She held out her hand for Cat to sniff. Cat stopped, sniffing it from a small distance, her heartbeat loud in her chest. The woman's fingers slowly lowered, and Cat remained still instead of running away. The fingers brushed past Cat's right ear, then feathered across the top of Cat's head.

Cat allowed the caress, then she wanted more. She pushed her head into the woman's palm. As the woman's fingers massaged her head, she began to purr.

The door opened again, and the woman's fingers stopped. The smell of meat wafted into the room. Cat tensed, but she didn't run away as the man stepped in, carrying a bowl that was the source of the smell.

Cat wanted to jump to the bowl, but the man stood next to it. Instead, Cat sat still and quivered.

The woman's fingers moved again as she murmured to Cat. By her dulcet tone, Cat was sure the woman was telling her how beautiful she was. How sleek her body was, how fast and nimble she was, and how wise she was.

"She's letting you pet her?" The man bent forward. "You're making progress."

Though it meant the woman couldn't pet her, Cat backed up, all the way under the bed again. The man was getting too close. Though her heart didn't pound in fear of him, she didn't wholly trust him.

The woman and the man spoke again. The woman stood and sighed. She said something to the man, and then she turned and hunched down to say something to Cat, a change in the woman's tone that Cat understood.

I'll care for you, the tone said. *I'll pet you. I'll feed you. I won't let you be cold ever again.*

The woman stood, then she and the man left, closing the door behind them.

Cat waited until she heard them reach the end of the hallway before she crept out from under the bed and padded to the bowl of food.

She gobbled the food down. For long days and long nights, she'd been hungry. For long days and long nights, she'd been cold. Cold that speared down into her bones. At least she'd had her mom and brother and sisters.

And then she'd lost them.

She feared that they'd frozen to death.

The food was in her belly now, filling it, and she went to sniff around the room. Everywhere she went, she smelled the woman's scent. She smelled the man's, too, but it wasn't as strong.

Finally, she jumped up on the bed and curled up. As she did, her tummy hurt. Something bad was happening to her. It had happened before, and she hadn't liked it.

She jumped off the bed onto the carpet.

Something was very wrong.

She wheezed, then she wheezed again, and she wheezed one more time. Her stomach felt like it was turning upside down.

"Ack. Ack. Ack."

Then her belly heaved.

Once.

Twice.

Three times.

Her back curved up, and her neck and head curved down. Then sour-smelling food hurled out of her mouth.

That done, she jumped up onto the bed again, perfectly fine now. The bed was soft, and the covers bunched up around her. Being here was like going to cat heaven.

If the lady gave her some of the food that smelled so good, Cat would love her forever.

"The house smells good." Avery's voice was sleepy.

Julian smiled. After the workout he'd just given her, he expected her to be wiped out. Before they created another story to add to his growing legend, he always had a burst of high-powered energy. Expending it with a woman was always the best way to get the edge off.

Now his mind was sharp, and while Avery napped, he was planning what he would do, to whom he would do it, and when he would do it.

They would eat first, though he didn't have much of an appetite now. Too excited to care about food, though that could change to a great hunger in a snap.

After the meal was over and everyone talked about how much they loved the meal and whatever bullshit holiday stuff they'd done, he would speak up, and he would tell them who he and Avery were.

He would see the dismay in their eyes.

He would see the fear.

Just thinking about it and picturing their frightened faces, the power grew inside of him.

Bigger and wider and hotter.

"You know what we need to do before we leave this place?" he asked.

"Hmmm?" Her eyes were closed, and her breathing was slowing into sleep.

"This is the longest we've stayed at a place before we've done our business."

She snorted a laugh, and her eyelids half opened. "*Done our business.* Like dogs doing their business. That's good."

He didn't smile back, but a buzz went through him. "Our fingerprints will be everywhere."

The smile wiped off her face. Her eyes opened.

"When we're done," he said, "we need to burn the place down."

Staring at him, she nodded. "Yes. Burn the place down."

He reached out to pat her head. Like she was a dog. His dog. "Good girl."

She closed her eyes again, and he watched as her breathing slowed and her facial muscles slackened. He inhaled deeply and could smell the turkey. Just a small scent curling up the stairway and into their room, but he had a great sense of smell. *Eat me,* it called to him. *Eat me.*

And he would, a surge of hunger starting now. He'd eat the turkey and all the other fixings. After that, while the others were in a turkey-and-stuffing stupor, he would be energized. Ready to kill them all.

Yes, after that, perhaps he would take out a few things he could stuff into their car. But mostly he didn't care about *things*. He didn't even care about the fame that would follow him, though it amused him. Entertained him. But he could live without it.

He cared about the fear. It was that look of horror on their faces that energized him.

The first time he'd seen that fear was on his third stepfather's face.

The torturer became the tortured.

It had been the first time in a long time that he'd felt happy.

Since then, he'd felt happy often.

As he closed his eyes, he smiled. Most people didn't know that life was a game, and everyone had their choice to be a loser or a winner. Because of their ignorance or their need to be *nice*—a word that made him want to throw up— most people were losers.

Not him. He was a winner all the way. When he finally died, he would be an old, old man, smiling at his memories.

Sixteen

DAYLIGHT WAS WANING as they passed the platters of food down the table, the scent of roasted turkey filling the dining room. Taylor and Erica had helped Sylvia set the table, though she could have done it herself in the same amount of time—or less—if they'd stayed out of her way. Now the couples shared bits about themselves. Letting each other know who they were. Probably, Sylvia thought, making themselves sound better than they really were.

Not that she blamed them. She certainly didn't tell anyone the truth about herself.

She listened as the couples spoke. Taylor and Brad were from Madison, while Nolan and Erica were from Jefferson County. Taylor and Brad were talking twice as much as Nolan and Erica. Sylvia had the feeling that something was bothering Nolan and Erica.

Nothing appeared to bother the other couple. Brad seemed like a regular guy, the kind that fit right in with the locals at the bar. And Taylor was the perky cheerleader type. When the table was set, and the food was on the table, Taylor took pictures of all of the food. And when they sat, she took pictures of them all, planning to post them on the different online places.

As she took her pictures, Brad smiled widely, clearly proud and supportive of his outgoing girlfriend. The kind of husband every woman wanted.

Though perhaps Sylvia's impressions were all wrong. Sylvia liked to think that she was good at reading people, but most of them showed their good sides and hid the bad.

After all, that's what she did.

She dismissed her thoughts as she took a scoop of sweet potato casserole, then passed it on to Nate. In any case, tomorrow morning the four guests would pack up and drive away. There would be just Nate and her staying here for a few more days. And Teela.

Thinking about it made her happy.

No, not happy. *Happier.*

She looked at Nate, and a revelation came to her. *He* made her happy. Since the first day she'd met him, she'd admired his intelligence, his kindness, his humor. He made her laugh. And in bed, he was the best lover she'd had, always making sure she was getting as much pleasure as he was.

All this time, she'd thought of him as someone she liked and respected. A friend. Their relationship had been the best she'd had with a man. There was no drama, no nervousness, no wild hammering of her heart, no doubts. No misery. All of the emotions she'd gone through with Charley.

She'd thought *that* had been real love.

Living with Nate hadn't been anything like that. She'd loved him as a person almost right from the beginning. It had been such an easy love. Easy to live with. Easy to make love with.

She hadn't thought real love could be so easy.

She'd been wrong. She loved Nate. *Loved him.* Not only love as a friend, or as a person, but love with every fiber of her being. With her whole heart.

And loving him as a friend wasn't so shabby, either. She trusted him, something she didn't do easily. Since she'd moved in with him, he'd proposed to her once a month.

The last time he'd proposed had been in October on his birthday. She'd told him not to ask her again, and he'd nodded, frowning slightly, his eyes sad.

It had been two months now since his last proposal.

He'd finally listened to her.

Stupid. She'd been so stupid.

She frowned at the cranberry relish on her plate. Maybe it wasn't stupid. Now *she* could propose to *him.* She'd do it as soon as this dinner was over and they were alone.

"Aren't you Jewish?" Taylor asked, passing the bowl of beans to Nate, who sat between her and Sylvia, with Sylvia at the end of the table. Nolan and Erica sat on the other long side of the table, while Brad sat at the other end.

Nate grinned at Taylor. "I don't have this nose for nothing."

"Yet you're celebrating Christmas."

"Actually, *you* might be celebrating Christmas by eating a turkey and other foods. Me, I'm enjoying a delicious meal with my favorite lady and four new friends. But it's fine by me that you're celebrating the birth of a young Jewish man who wanted to feed the hungry and sometimes sat down to dinner with prostitutes and thieves."

Erica laughed, her normal somber expression lighting up her face, and Brad darted her a look of appreciation.

"I'm agnostic," Nolan said. "Yet I'm also enjoying the meal."

"I'm not agnostic, but I also enjoy a delicious meal." Erica smiled at Sylvia. "Thank you for inviting us. This could have turned into a disastrous holiday, but you made it into a wonderful one that I'll always remember."

Nolan reached under the table, as if he were squeezing his wife's thigh. "Me, too. Until the day I die."

Erica stared at him, and for a moment there was a stillness in the air. As if time stood still.

Sylvia shivered, and she didn't know why.

"I didn't mean to offend anyone," Taylor said, her voice pitched high like a little girl's. "I didn't mean anything."

"No offense taken." Nate picked up a fork. "You asked a question, and I answered. It reminded me of my students."

The others laughed but not Sylvia. She didn't dislike Taylor, but she found her a little tiresome.

"If anyone wants to say a prayer before we

eat"—Nate glanced around the table—"I won't be offended with that, either."

Nolan and Erica looked at each other, and the intensity on their faces made Sylvia shiver again and turn to the other couple. Brad was looking at Taylor, and there was just something in his face, like a small boy about to commit mischief, that made Sylvia raise her eyebrows.

Usually she was the observer. Tonight, though, she felt as if she was a player and an observer at the same time.

She wasn't sure she liked it.

"Health and happiness to all," Brad said, looking around at everyone.

"And good food." Nate gestured at the loaded plates. "Eat. Drink. Be merry."

"I'm all for that." Taylor dug her fork into the stuffing. "This all looks so yummy."

A plaintive meow came from the hallway where their bedroom was, loud enough for them all to hear.

Sylvia got to her feet and put her napkin on the chair. "If you'll excuse me for a minute."

Nate looked at her, his eyebrows up. She hurried away. The best thing about reaching her fifties was that she no longer felt the need to explain herself to others.

In seconds, she was in her room. Teela lay on the bed, and when Sylvia reached over to pet her, Teela backed up, looking ready to jump away if Sylvia moved an inch closer.

There was puke on the faded carpet.

She turned and headed to the bathroom for a rag and anything else she'd need.

It only took a few minutes to clean up as the cat watched her. She made two trips back to the bathroom, and then she was done.

"You're not making this easy." In the bedroom again, Sylvia bent forward and talked to the cat on the bed as it warily watched her. "That's okay. I'm not easy, either. I suppose you want turkey now. Is the smell driving you crazy? We'll have leftovers, but if you puke again, I'll have to stop giving you human food."

She turned away, because there was another reason she'd hurried to the bedroom. The real reason she hadn't ignored the plaintive meow.

Something had felt wrong at the table. Something about the way the two couples looked at each other. Something that made her fingers tingle. If her arms hadn't been covered by the red-and-green Christmas sweater that Chuck had left in a gift bag on her dresser, she thought that the hairs on her arms might have stood on end.

Perhaps because of what had happened last Christmas, she was overly anxious. After all, it wasn't likely that someone would attempt to kill her again. She didn't know these people, so there was no reason for any of them to hate her. And they certainly wouldn't hate Nate, who was just so...well, *loveable*. Or, for most people, likeable.

And the guests seemed normal. As normal as any person could be.

Maybe she was the one who was crazy, because she opened her closet, pushed aside some clothes, and opened a small safe. Her Beretta 21A Bobcat was new, an early Christmas gift she'd bought for herself.

She loaded the pistol, then slid the Beretta into her sweater pocket, where it fit easily. Stepping back, she closed the safe, then shifted the clothes on hangers to hide it from the casual eye. She was taking ridiculous cautions, which was another part of her mild OCD. But the minute she didn't do this, it would matter.

Only then did she close the closet door and head over to Teela, who watched her carefully, still not completely trusting her. Leaning on the bed, Sylvia said, "I'll be back in a couple of hours. I promise to bring you turkey."

As she turned to leave the bedroom, she noted that she was walking taller, her step swifter and more sure. She always felt in control with a gun so close at hand. So easy to slip her hand in her pocket and draw the Beretta out. Then click off the safety, aim, and shoot.

Much easier than throwing a turkey at the offender, which was what had happened last year. No one had been harmed at the time—if she didn't count the turkey.

She didn't believe the turkey would be in harm's way today. She hoped that *no one* was going to be harmed. That it would be a joyous celebration, and a good time was to be had by all.

And when it was over, and she and Nate were alone in their bedroom, maybe she would give him her real present—if she didn't chicken out. Or if he didn't chicken out. And she would do it without a weapon.

Because some things weren't good to do with a gun in her hand.

Seventeen

SHE WAS GONE too long. Did she suspect something?

The minute the thought entered Julian's mind, he dismissed it. Perhaps he'd imagined trouble because so far it had been so easy. Not just now, but every time. A little trouble might be a pleasant change. It would add a challenge to his plan. Put some spice into the pot.

The thought excited him, giving him a hard-on for a smart opponent. A worthy opponent.

Just before death, his victims always had an astonished look in their wide-open eyes. A shocked look, as if they'd seen in that one second what he really was.

The devil. Evil. Not a modern-day Clyde, with Avery as his Bonnie. Unlike the two depression-era, gun-toting killers, he and Avery didn't plan to die in a hail of bullets.

The others were talking and nodding, and he nodded along with them.

The Jew was looking at the hallway, and it was clear to Julian that he had a big hard-on for Sylvia. Not because they were a couple but because of the way he looked at her. She was his weak spot. His Kryptonite.

That was too bad. With his sharp wit, Nate could have been a worthy opponent. But love dragged a man down, distracted a man, weakened him. Making Nate as vulnerable as the rest of humanity who looked at Julian and saw a good-looking man who dressed as most men his age dressed and spoke well. Because of these superficialities, they assumed he was a good person. After all, he wasn't scruffy or glowering or muttering under his breath with spittle spraying out of his mouth. He didn't even sport any tattoos. He wasn't perfect, but he was normal. And normal was better than perfect. Especially for a hunter seeking his prey.

Avery leaned slightly toward Julian. With her hand below the table, she reached over his thigh and a little farther yet. Finding his fly. Squeezing.

He half closed his eyes as she squeezed again. And again. And again.

Good. Good. Good.

With a deep inhale, he gripped her wrist and forced her hand off of his lap.

Later they would do this. After the others were all dead. Blood seeping out of their lacerated skin. Heads conked down on their dessert plates.

Or perhaps they would be sliding sideways, falling against each other. Toppling to the side and tumbling onto the floor.

So many possibilities.

Smiling, he picked up a forkful of cranberries with sliced almonds, spiced with cinnamon and sugar. Just the way he liked it.

He wished Sylvia would return for her last supper. She should enjoy the food, which was very good. It was only polite that he thank her before she died.

Sylvia returned to the dining room, her hand in her right pocket to make sure no one saw the gun's outline. She was ninety-nine percent positive it would be invisible to everyone, but she wasn't the kind of person who took chances. The reason that, so far, no one suspected her of murder.

"Are you all right?" Nate asked. "And the cat?"

Seated, she picked up her fork. "I'm fine. I just wanted to make sure Teela was all right."

"You have a great heart."

"It's Christmas." She looked at him, because she didn't want to lie. "It's cold out," she added, because it was really nothing to do with Christmas. "If the weather were warmer, I'd probably leave her to forage."

"You would?" Taylor stared at her, her eyes wide and her mouth half open.

Sylvia glanced around. Erica was frowning at her, too. Huh! *City* girls.

"If it were one of the other three seasons," she said, "Teela wouldn't have been in my garage. She would have probably been outside pouncing on a mouse or a squirrel. She would have been able to find her own food."

"It's terrible, honey." Brad patted the back of Taylor's hand on the table. "But she's right."

Taylor's lips pouted. She could have been a lipstick model with her shapely lips. "Maybe it's a woman thing, but I just couldn't leave a cute little kitty outside without trying to save it."

Brad turned to Erica. "What do you think?"

"Me?" Her eyebrows rose, and she shrugged her thin shoulders beneath her silver-threaded sweater. "Whatever I'd say now would be the easy answer. But whatever I'd actually do might not match my answer."

Nate chuckled. "Bingo. The perfect answer."

Nolan gazed at Erica, a smile in his dark eyes. "My wife is smart and beautiful."

"So, you agree with her?" Brad said.

"With my wife or with Sylvia?" Nolan's smile disappeared. "I was raised on a farm, and all I can say is that if you want to catch an outdoor cat in any season but winter, good luck with that."

"You think it can't be done?" Taylor leaned forward over the table.

"Of course it can be done," Nolan said. "But not easily."

"The good things in life are never easy," Nate said.

Watching the group, Sylvia had the unsettling feeling that the other five—including Nate—were verbally sparring as they ate. These weren't her usual guests sitting around her table, who'd come here to relax and enjoy themselves. To *chill out,* she might say if it were summer instead of winter. During Christmas, most of their guests came to have a cozy and old-fashioned holiday.

This was not normal.

112

Maybe that was the real reason she'd snuck the gun in her pocket. The sense that something was out of whack.

After all she'd gone through, she'd equated *not normal* with *killing*, which showed how off-balance her life had become.

This whole dinner felt off-balance. Wrong. Like a scene from an old British mystery novel in which everyone at the dinner table was a stranger to the others. The conversation was dry and witty, with each of them eating the same dishes. But somewhere in the middle, one of them would die of food poisoning. No one knew why or how or who until either the detective with the waxed mustache or the old lady from the village added four and five and came up with one murderer.

Nate leaned over to her. "You're not eating."

"I was just thinking," she said.

"Anything special?"

"I was thinking..." Glancing around, she saw that everyone was watching her. She swallowed, then continued, "That this conversation might be the most interesting we've ever had at this dinner table. Not just the conversation but the guests, too."

"Even me?" Taylor giggled.

Sylvia stared at her. Yes, even Taylor. Was Taylor so stupid she didn't know that?

Or was Taylor really a smart woman? One who wanted people to think she was less intelligent than she really was?

Perhaps Brad preferred his women not as smart as he was, though he didn't seem that way.

But how a man acted in private was often different from his public self.

"She sees through you, darling." Brad smiled at Taylor, and her face lit up. As if she would treasure any crumb of a compliment that he sent her.

Something about the adoration in Taylor's eyes made Sylvia feel a little sick. She never liked those sick games that people played with each other. She liked honesty—though if she were honest with Nate, he would probably race out of the house, jump in his car, and speed away.

She wouldn't blame him. If he told her that he'd murdered people who pissed him off, she might run as fast as she could, too.

Or not. If that happened—though she knew it wouldn't—she might ask him what kind of a gun he'd used.

The guests had gone silent, and she realized they were staring at her. She cleared her throat. "Is everyone ready for dessert?"

The sooner they were done with the meal, the happier she would be.

Eighteen

THE GUESTS HELPED clear the table. Julian followed Sylvia and Nate to the kitchen. It amused Julian that Sylvia walked swiftly with Nate close behind her, like a male dog following a female dog in heat. Though Sylvia was older than Julian, she was still a splendid creature with her wavy blond hair and patrician facial features. If she had decided to be an actress instead of an innkeeper, she would never have been short of roles.

In the kitchen, Avery nudged him in his ribs. "Are you actually staring at her?" she asked, her voice low.

"Are you actually jealous?"

"Since I know this isn't going to have a good ending for her," she said in her low voice, "no, I'm not."

He glanced at the other two guests, who were talking to each other in low voices, too.

A thought struck him. What if they were also planning on murder and mayhem? What if they had stuck a gun in their waistband, waiting for the perfect moment to use it?

He held back a laugh. The other two had their agenda, but that wasn't it. Whatever their plan was, it didn't matter. Not to him. And certainly not to them, though they didn't know it yet. The only plan that mattered was his, because when this was over, only two people would walk out of here: Avery and him.

He wouldn't even spare the cat.

"Relax." He picked up the dessert forks. He was playing the role of the good guest. "Enjoy the day. After all, it's Christmas."

She slapped her hand over her mouth and giggled.

He smirked. For her Christmas present, he would let her choose anything she wanted from the house that she could fit into the car.

Before they burned the house down.

He took her hand in his and squeezed it. "Life is good, baby."

She gazed into his eyes. "I love you so much that if you left me, I would die."

He didn't say anything, because he knew what she said was true. In fact, before he ever left her, he would make sure she was dead.

He had one motto in life: leave no witnesses. Not a mouse. Not a cat. And definitely not a woman.

The humans were in the kitchen, their voices loud, like blows to Cat's ears. Cat could hear Sylvia's voice, too. But Cat liked Sylvia's voice, especially when she spoke softly. Almost like a purr. Cat already recognized a few words. *Food. Eat. Pretty kitty.*

But the other voices were pitched wrong. Too high. Too excited. And one of them spoke too smoothly. Cat liked smoothness, but this was smooth like a snake was smooth, just before it struck.

Cat jumped off the bed, where she'd curled up on a pillow that smelled like Sylvia, and she landed on the floor with a soft plunk that only cats could hear. The door was open the width of her whiskers, and she padded to it.

If she wanted to, she could work it open wider. But she didn't want to. The wrongly pitched voices scared her as much as a screech of a hungry crow.

Cat's body stilled with alertness.

It wasn't just one voice that made her nervous. It was two.

She didn't like this. She didn't like it at all.

Why weren't the humans noticing the bad voices? How come Sylvia didn't hear?

Cat mewled, a pitiful, scared sound.

When no one came, she knew that no human had heard her.

"Something's wrong with Teela." Sylvia twisted toward the hallway leading to her bedroom. "Did you hear that? It sounded like a moan."

"Teela's fine." Nate cupped his hand around her shoulder. "And if something's wrong with her, you can't do anything about it tonight. Didn't you say the local vet was visiting relatives in Michigan?"

She nodded. "I wish she'd come back soon."

"So you could find someone to adopt Teela?"

She didn't answer. She just breathed in and out.

"Sylvia?" His voice nudged her to talk.

"Something about Teela reminds me of myself."

From the living room came a burst of laughter, but there was silence in the kitchen for the time it took her to inhale and exhale twice.

"You want to keep her after all?"

"I'm thinking about it. I've grown..."

"You love her," he said.

"Accustomed to her meow."

"We were planning on traveling to California in the summer."

"I can ask Chuck and Raine to take care of her for a few weeks. They would do it."

"I like cats. I like all animals. If that's what you want, I'm fine with it." He turned to the counter where the apple and the pumpkin pies sat, looking almost too perfect to eat.

Her throat clenched with emotion. She had the feeling that if she said she wanted to keep a death adder as a pet, he'd shrug and say, *Whatever you want, I'm fine with it.*

"Did you notice a funny vibe in the dining room?" Nate turned to her, holding a pie in each hand as well as any seasoned waiter.

He'd never looked so sexy.

Was that a good reason to say yes to marriage? A man who helped in the kitchen?

Probably eighty percent of the single women she knew would say, *Hell yes.*

"I wouldn't call the vibe funny. *I'm* not laughing about it." Sylvia opened the refrigerator and brought out the bowl of whipping cream for the pumpkin pie. "Let's go. Time for the last course."

"Last course sounds so final." Nate nodded at her to go ahead of him. "Like Jesus's last supper."

Walking away, she thought that they'd all have a last supper sometime. She hoped hers would be as good as today's—but not yet. She had plans for the time ahead of her.

Marriage to Nate. It sounded...so good that it scared her.

Nineteen

THERE WERE GROANS, and both couples said they couldn't eat any more. Yet everyone but Nolan had room for a piece of pie. After they were done, the couples sat for a couple minutes without speaking, in a turkey and pie stupor.

"That was one of the best meals I've had." Brad patted his stomach.

"Thank you," Sylvia said. "It's probably the same meal you'll find throughout Trouble Bay, either last night or today."

"My mother always makes a turkey dinner for Christmas." Erica held up her glass of wine, a salute to Sylvia. "I love my mom, but her dinners aren't half as good as yours."

Sylvia dipped her chin in acknowledgment. "I'm glad you enjoyed the meal."

"It was *perfect.*" Taylor smiled brightly, sitting straight, her eyes bright and energetic—apparently recovered from the surfeit of food.

In that second, Sylvia hated her. Unlike the younger woman, Sylvia was too full to do much more tonight than put the dishes in the dishwasher, pet Teela—if Teela allowed petting—and snuggle up to Nate.

Nate leaned toward her. "Every meal with you," he said for her ears only, "is perfect."

Tears unexpectedly stung her eyes. She didn't know why. He wasn't stingy with his compliments, and he praised her often.

Maybe today she just finally believed him. Maybe today she finally realized she might be good enough for him.

"It's perfect with you, too," she said, her voice low.

He stared at her, and she laughed, though it came out as a half sob. She put her hand on his cheek and nodded, then turned to the table as euphoria filled her.

All that weird stuff she'd been feeling before about her guests was gone. There'd been nothing wrong with them. The only thing wrong had been with her, with her own suspicious mind.

She needed therapy. Someone to figure out *why* her first instinct wasn't to appreciate her boyfriend. Oh, no, her first instinct was to run to a safe in her bedroom, where she kept her guns and her ammunition.

More than that, someone should convince her that she was crazy to keep a small arsenal in a hidden compartment in her clothes closet.

Yes, she had saved lives, but that was over.

And she'd already run into homicidal maniacs twice in her life. How likely was it that she would run into a third maniac?

The only homicidal maniac in this place might be herself.

She pushed that thought away. She was done with regrets. She was done with self-recriminations. No more, no more, no more.

A smile widened on Nate's face as he stared at her. "Does this mean what I think it does?"

"Yes."

"You'll marry me?"

She laughed loudly. None of the others were talking, and she was sure they were watching her and Nate. Normally she'd hate that knowledge. Hate their eyes on her.

Now she didn't care what thoughts were going through their minds. "Yes," she said, loudly and clearly. "I love you, Nate, and it's time we made it legal."

He beamed. "Then let's clean up and—"

"We'll clean up for you." Erica stood, and Sylvia was surprised to see tears in her eyes. "It's the least we can do."

Taylor stood, too. "I agree. It's the least we can all do."

Sylvia had to hold back a grimace. She appreciated the offer, but how could she tell them that she didn't want them to manhandle her dishes? And how would they know where to put them?

They would have no idea where the containers were that she used to store the food. And she didn't want them poking into her cupboards and handling her dishes and glasses. They'd been drinking wine! The wine glasses needed to be hand-washed, and they might put them in the dishwasher.

Just thinking about it, she felt her blood pressure rising.

"No, really, I—"

"Don't be silly." Taylor giggled. "We're doing the dishes, and that's that."

Silly? Sylvia pressed her lips together to keep from saying words that no one had ever heard her say. "Thank you, but I can't allow you to do that." She stood and started to turn to Nate—

"Don't worry about the dishes." Brad stood, and his voice had changed from friendly to commanding, his right hand slightly behind him. "As it turns out, you won't need to worry about them."

Before anyone could ask him what he was talking about, he casually shifted his arm, lifting it, so they could all see the gun in his hand. A revolver. Sylvia could tell by the revolving cylinder above the trigger. With enough shots to kill all of them.

Twenty

SYLVIA'S SENSES CAME alive, the way she imagined a small animal in a forest would become alert as it hid from the fox. Next to her, on her left, Nate gripped the dessert fork. As if he was going to use it as a weapon.

On the right of her peripheral vision, she saw Nolan place his hand on the back of Erica's hand. With his other hand, slightly to his left, he gripped Sylvia's favorite Stoneware pie plate.

He was going to try to be a hero.

She swiftly turned her gaze to the other couple. Brad was smiling now. Not talking but glancing around as if he were an actor who expected to be applauded for his role.

He *relished* what he was doing. The thought frightened Sylvia more than the revolver in his hand.

In another sense, it comforted her. It made what she'd done in the past not as evil. When she'd killed, she'd never felt happy. She'd never felt proud. She'd always known what she'd done was wrong.

And after the murders, she hadn't thrived

because of what she'd done. Instead, she'd shrunk into herself, and she'd tried to be perfect. As if being perfect would make up for what she'd done. An impossible task, since she was human, and no human was perfect.

And now, just as she was poking her head out of her self-imposed cocoon, this crazed maniac was going to kill her. Kill Nate. Kill Erica and Nolan.

At first, she hadn't cared for the couple, but now she did. Especially in comparison to this grinning egomaniac and his giggling girlfriend.

All these thoughts passed through her mind in seconds.

"You're the couple from Michigan," Erica said.

"That's us," Brad said in a deepened *I am God* voice.

Sylvia clenched her jaw. She hated that kind of male voice. Always voiced by someone who thought he was omnipotent. She liked to think that if she ever met God, he would greet her with such compassion and love—and forgiveness—in his voice and his shining eyes that it would make her weep with joy.

"Why us?" Erica glanced around the table. "I don't think you'll find a lot of money here."

"It's not about the money this time," he said.

"What is it then?" Erica held her head up, her shoulders stiff, and Brad's blue eyes ran over her. As if he were appraising an object of art.

He's going to rape Erica before killing her.

Then he turned his gaze to Sylvia.

And I'll be next.

If he could get it up for both her and Erica.

Though if he were in a manic stage, she suspected it was possible.

She didn't freeze with fear or feel hot with anger. Her mind was clear. Her emotions calm.

Good. She didn't want him to see fear in her face. He was a psychopath. A man who used the force of his personality to charm people. To gain their trust. And when he shot bullets into their hearts, it brought him satisfaction. Perhaps even joy. He fed on fear.

She didn't want him to see any emotion or thought in her face. She wasn't giving him ammunition to feed his twisted ego.

Taylor said something to Brad, calling him *Julian,* which must be his real name. Demanding his attention, if only for a moment or a few seconds. Sylvia could feel her jealousy that he even looked at her, a woman who was more than twenty years his senior.

Not taking her eyes off of him, Sylvia slid her hand into her sweater pocket.

At the same time, she saw—no, felt—Nate slide his arm off the table.

"Don't do it," Brad/Julian said.

Sylvia froze, but he was staring at Nate, not at her.

That's when she noticed Nate's hands were beneath the table. When she realized he had planned to push the table upward and toward Brad/Julian.

Nate smiled as he kept his attention on Brad/Julian, and an icy fear ran through Sylvia.

"If you try anything..." Brad/Julian kept his gaze on Nate, but he angled the gun toward her, the aim astonishingly accurate, though she thought she could duck and avoid it while bringing her gun up to shoot him.

It might not work, but she would be faster.

Did it matter?

Whatever she did, there was a big possibility that before it was over, she and Nate would be dead.

Something was wrong. Cat crouched inside the bedroom by the door. Something had changed. The air carried vibrations, like just before a bad storm came. Only this was worse than snow. Worse than a rainstorm.

Something to do with the humans. The dining room where the humans ate was a short way from the bedroom, and she could hear someone talking. A man's voice. A *cold* voice. Cold like snow, the kind with ice crystals that hurt her paws and legs. A cold that made her think she would die.

Sylvia, the human who had brought Cat into the warm house and had fed her and whom Cat had allowed to pet her for a short moment, was scared. Cat could smell the scent of fear. Not one scent but different scents.

It reminded Cat of the way she'd felt when the cold weather had come, and the barn had fallen down, crashing around them, leaving her in the frigid wind that seemed to blow right through her while she'd run as fast and as far as she could, looking for her family. Looking for shelter.

Until Cat couldn't run anymore with the cold hurting her feet, her stomach empty, and she was so weak that she wanted to curl up to sleep and never wake up. She'd been ready to lie down in the snow when the building opened up, and she'd raced inside.

Then Sylvia had found Cat and taken her into the house. She'd fed her and had given her water. She didn't force her to do anything. Instead, Sylvia had talked softly to her, like a mother bird calling softly to its baby bird.

Who would take care of her if something bad happened to Sylvia?

Cat didn't know what she could do to help Sylvia, but she had to do something.

Trembling, Cat squeezed through the small opening, her body pushing the door open wider. She padded down the hall, quieter than a mouse, then stuck her head into the dining room.

A man was talking, his back to her. His voice was smooth but not a good smooth. It was smooth like the swish of a big bird's wing as it flew after its prey.

Smooth like the sound of a snake slithering through the grass and the weeds.

Smooth that made the fur on Cat's spine rise.

A need to do something that didn't come from bravery but from survival roared up inside Cat.

If the man killed Sylvia, he would kill Cat, too.

She sprang up, her claws out, catching on the man's sweater.

The man snapped around, and so did the woman next to him. "The cat!" she screeched. "The fucking cat!"

Twenty-one

IT HAPPENED QUICKLY. Sylvia saw the small, tiger-striped tabby leap up at Brad. Brad's head jerked back, his hands flinging up.

Sylvia lowered her gun to just below the tabletop. She couldn't shoot a moving target. She might shoot Teela instead of Brad.

From the corner of her eye, she saw Nolan stand, his hand up, over his shoulder. Then he threw a wine bottle at Brad, just as Brad shoved Teela off of him.

The bottle bounced off of the back of Brad's head and smashed onto the table, pouring red wine onto the tablecloth and Sylvia's good dishes. Brad shifted to face the table, his left hand pressed against his forehead and his eyes narrowed at Nolan. "You're a fucking dead man," he said.

Sylvia raised her gun again, but Brad's gun was already aimed at Nolan as he pulled the trigger, the sudden bang reverberating in the dining room as Nolan toppled, falling toward Erica. She screamed, catching him before he fell off of the chair.

Taylor laughed.

Brad smiled.

Sylvia's eyes narrowed as she pulled the trigger.

The blast was sudden, but she was prepared for the kick as Brad slid downward, his face turned toward her, his eyes surprised.

Sylvia watched the life force ooze out of him, his face blanking and his eyes staring into nothingness. She recognized that look of death. She'd seen it too often.

Nate grabbed the gun.

Taylor screamed, a wailing sound, as if she'd lost her only friend.

It all happened in seconds, and Sylvia stared at the two couples. The two men. Brad dead. She knew that, because she'd seen the bullet hit him between the eyes. A perfect shot.

Nolan...she wasn't sure. Erica was crying out Brad's name, but Sylvia didn't know if she was in shock or in the beginning of grief.

Sylvia turned to Nate, but he was keeping his eyes on Taylor. Good. She twisted to gaze at Nolan again. Erica was bending over him, tears tracking down her face.

"Heal for me, sweetheart." Erica's voice cracked. "Heal. Don't die now. Please, don't die." She sobbed, her arms around him.

Sylvia's eyes burned with the beginning of tears. Turning her gaze from Nolan to Brad's still body, she didn't feel guilty. Not one ounce of guilt. She was glad he was dead. Fiercely glad.

If she had to relive these last five minutes over again, she would do the same thing again in a second.

"One of us has to call the sheriff," Nate said.

She blinked, giving him her attention. It was clear that he wasn't returning her gun. Since he was in control of the situation, she pushed away from the table. Her cell phone was in the kitchen. As she walked there, her legs felt rubbery. She grabbed her phone from the counter, and her hands were trembling as she clicked on the three numbers. She walked back to stare into the dining room, relieved as a nine-one-one operator answered the phone.

Her voice shook only a little as she told the operator their location and said that a guest had been shot and was severely injured. He needed an ambulance right *now*.

Another man was dead, she added, hearing the change in her voice. The flatness. "I believe he's the murderer from Michigan. His female accomplice is in my dining room."

After confirming her address again, Sylvia hung up and called Pete Masters, the sheriff's deputy who lived in Trouble Bay, and quickly told him what had happened.

"Oh, boy," he said. "Oh, boy, oh, boy. I'll be there in two minutes."

She hung up and watched the tears trail down Erica's face as she bent over Nolan. His blue sweater was soaked with blood on the left side of his chest. Sylvia couldn't tell if he was alive or dead.

And then she heard the rasp of his breath, as if he were fighting for each inhale and exhale.

"You saved my life." Erica's lips and her voice trembled. "Please don't die yet. I'm not ready to let you go." She whispered hoarsely, "Wherever you go, even death, I want to be with you."

Sylvia said a silent prayer for them.

"No." Nolan's voice was a croak.

Erica leaned closer to him. Blood spotted her light blue sweater, and there was a blood smear on her face.

"*You*." The word was a hoarse whisper, and Nolan's eyes were glued to Erica's. "Live. For. You. Promise me."

"Oh, my bossy love." Tears tracked down Erica's face. "You win. But when I finally get to heaven, you better be there, waiting for me."

Nolan closed his eyes as Erica held his hand, and there was just the sound of his rasping breath and Taylor's weeping.

Nate still held the gun aimed at Taylor. Sylvia hoped he didn't have to shoot her, but if he did, she would back him up and say it was an accident.

She leaned toward Nate. "I have a Taser. You want me to get it?"

"You're actually asking me?" He glanced at her, then quickly returned his attention to Taylor.

Sylvia nodded, feeling slightly surprised. "Yes, I am asking you."

"I don't think that's a good idea."

As she nodded, Taylor's wailing grew louder. Sylvia reached for the half-filled pitcher of ice water still on the table and raised it.

"What about pouring this on her head?"

"No!" Taylor screamed. "No, you bitch!"

"Shut up, or I will. In a second."

Taylor's eyes shot hatred at Sylvia, but her wailing stopped.

Erica lifted her head. "Thank you."

The doorbell rang. Sylvia stood. "That must be Pete. I'll be right back."

As she hurried to the living room, she knew that after today, all their lives would be changed.

She pulled the front door open and gestured Pete inside. The deputy was a friend of her son's, but he looked younger with his roundish baby face. "The body's in the dining room," she said. "I think you know where it is."

He stomped his booted feet on the hall rug, knocking off the snow. "This is becoming a bad habit, Mrs. Pascal. People being killed in your house."

"The last time, no one was killed. Just knocked down by a turkey," Sylvia said, then winced as Pete slapped his hand over his mouth to muffle a guffaw. She hadn't meant to be humorous. She'd just stated a fact.

She stared sternly at Pete. "Lately it seems as if there are a lot of crazies in town."

"At least you're alive and unhurt," Pete said. "Your boyfriend, too. I'm glad about that."

The sound of a siren was coming from the south, and he glanced in that direction, then put his head down and hurried across her living room in his damp boots. Usually so meticulous about her carpet, she didn't even wince.

Twenty-two

SYLVIA AND NATE answered Pete's questions. They answered for Erica, too. She had no eyes for anyone but Nolan, her concentration on him as she whispered over and over, *"Don't die, Nolan. Don't die on me."*

In less than ten minutes the ambulance pulled up in front of their bed-and-breakfast. Right after it were two sheriff's car. The ambulance responders wouldn't allow Erica to come with them, but Sergeant Hanser, a stocky man with graying hair and eyebrows that resembled caterpillars, told a female deputy to drive her to the hospital.

That left Hanser, Pete, Sylvia, and Nate.

Sylvia told her story. Since she'd already told Pete what happened, it didn't hurt her. Or else, she was numb by tonight's events.

When Hanser asked why she'd brought the gun to the dinner table, she said, "I just had a weird feeling."

"The conversation had turned odd," Nate said.

"They sounded phony," she said. "They gave me the creeps."

"They were asking inappropriate questions," Nate said.

"Anything specific?" Hanser asked.

"Um…" She looked at Nate, then back at Hanser, opening her hands. "I can't specify anything they said or did. It was more their tone than anything else."

"A mocking tone," Nate said. "Like they knew something we didn't know."

Sylvia nodded. "Secretly laughing at us, only they didn't hide it well."

Hanser nodded, then turned to Nate. "The Beretta was Mrs. Pascal's gun, but *you* used it."

"I pulled it out—" Sylvia began.

"Then she froze," Nate said.

Sylvia stared at him. In her whole life, she'd *never* frozen while shooting a gun.

"She's a much better shot than I am." Nate leaned forward. "Since I killed a man, I hate to say that I was lucky, but that's what it was. He shot one man, and he'd planned to kill all of us."

"You two were *very* lucky you listened to that voice in your head." Hanser sat back, his belly pouching over his belt. "He and his crazy girlfriend were bad people."

Nate looked at her, and she looked back at him. Before Taylor—or Avery, as they knew her real name now—had burst into tears and asked for a lawyer, she'd told Pete they'd planned to kill all of them.

And then there was the physical proof. *Nolan.* Barely alive. Sylvia wasn't much on praying, but she kept sending prayers that Nolan would live, though Erica had told them that Nolan was being slowly crippled by a neurological disease that had no cure.

"You know you can't stay here tonight," Hanser said.

Pete gave them a sympathetic nod.

Sylvia frowned. On the TV murder mysteries, the house owners didn't have to move out.

"This isn't a TV murder," Hanser said, as if he were reading her mind. "There was a murder and an attempted murder here."

"An attempted *massacre*," Nate said.

Hanser nodded. "We know it was self-defense, but we still have to do our job. The snow stopped about a half hour ago, and you should be able to drive, as long as you're careful and don't drive too fast. Can't you find another place to stay? Maybe with a neighbor?"

"You don't need to go through the whole house, do you?" Sylvia felt a little sick inside at the thought.

"Since everything happened in the dining room, I believe we can confine it to that area and their suite. But I'm afraid you'll still have to leave."

"My cat. What about my cat?"

Hanser frowned. "I haven't seen a cat. Could it have run out when my deputies opened the door?"

"I doubt it. We rescued her two days ago." She took in a deep breath. "Teela was actually instrumental in saving our lives. Brad—or Julian—was going to shoot me, and she jumped up onto his back and distracted him."

"A fighter cat." Hanser chuckled. "My favorite kind."

Sylvia forced a smile. "My fighter cat is probably hiding under the bed right now, shaking with nerves. We were just starting to bond. I don't want to leave her alone."

"By all means, take your cat with you."

"I'll have to buy a carrier tomorrow." Sylvia fought to keep her eyes open. She was so tired.

"My mom has one in the basement," Pete said. "If it's okay with with Sergeant Hanser—"

"Go get it." Hanser nodded. "After all, it sounds like the cat's the real hero of this story."

Thirty minutes later, Sylvia and Nate walked out of the B and B with a squalling, frightened cat in an old carrier that had been in a basement for over a decade. Their suitcases, the litter box, and the cat's food and water dishes were in the back of Nate's car already, and Sylvia had called her old friend to reserve a room at his resort a mile away.

As they drove slowly to the resort, the tension eased out of her.

Once again, she'd gotten away with murder.

She closed her eyes. It wasn't over yet. She needed to sleep a good six to eight hours. After that, she needed to talk to Nate. She needed to find out what he knew and how long he'd known...and what he planned to do with that knowledge.

Just a short time ago, she'd thought about marrying him. Now she was wondering if she could trust him.

Twenty-three

FIRST THING AFTER breakfast the next morning, Sylvia and Nate drove to the hospital, only to find out that Nolan had passed away a half hour ago.

"His wife—" Sylvia started to say.

"You're friends?" the chirpy receptionist asked. "I can ask if anyone knows where she is. This is such a sad time."

Sylvia agreed that they were friends and she wanted to talk to Nolan's wife. The receptionist told them that the wife was in the chapel waiting for family members.

They thanked her and took the elevator. Sylvia's heart felt heavy, and she held Nate's hand.

It was luck and a miracle they were all alive.

The chapel had stained glass windows and muted lighting. Erica sat on the pew in the front, facing the altar. She turned to look up at them, and Sylvia thought how much Erica resembled the Virgin Mary, though with shorter hair.

She bent to hug Erica. "Nolan loved you. He was a great man."

Erica's face scrunched, holding back tears. "He

was a Marine before we married. Did you know that?"

Sylvia sat on her left. "I didn't know."

"Long before he died, he would have lost the power of his limbs." Tears trickled down her cheeks. "When he threw that bottle at Brad or whatever his name was—"

"Satan," Nate said.

Erica hiccupped, a half-sob, half-laugh. "He knew what would happen. If he'd been able to say more than a few words, he would have said it was a good way to die."

Sylvia put her arm around Erica's back, and Erica sobbed quietly on Sylvia's shoulder.

The door opened. A couple about Sylvia's age and two women who looked to be in their twenties rushed into the room. "Sweetheart!" the older woman called.

Erica raised her head, getting to her feet, then stumbling. The two younger women reached her first, catching her and hugging her. Both of them had Erica's coloring and height. The older couple came behind them, tears streaming down their faces. The two younger women were wailing, too.

Sylvia took Nate's hand. They looked at each other, not saying a word, then walked out of the chapel.

When they reached the parking lot, sunlight bounced off of the pristine new snowfall. Though they'd only been in the hospital a little more than twenty minutes, it was cold inside Nate's car. As they headed to Trouble Bay, the heater blasted, car heating up quickly.

Nate took the shore road instead of Highway

42, the Subaru passing houses with views of the bay. "Would you like to live in one of these houses?" he asked.

She didn't answer right away. Part of her was still mourning Nolan. She hadn't known him well, but he'd died a hero.

"We'd have a beautiful view," she said, and heard the hoarseness of her voice, "but the lake homes are expensive and taxes are crazy."

"I have money. I can afford it."

"Is that what you want?" She turned to look at him.

"If that's what *you* want, I would do it."

"Except for this last year, I've lived in one house my whole life." She spoke slowly, because if she talked too fast, she thought her voice might tremble. "I'm not ready to move back here. Not permanently. I'd still like to visit Trouble Bay, of course. Chuck and Raine plan on making their main home in Trouble Bay, so I might want to rent a place when I visit. Maybe I could buy a condo."

"Especially if you have grandchildren," Nate said.

She laughed and was surprised that she could. "Especially then."

"I like the idea of buying a condo," Nate said. "When we're not using it, we might even rent it out."

At the word *we*, she tensed. As if Nate sensed this, he turned on the radio, a jazz song with no words. She was grateful, as most jazz songs had either sad or sexy lyrics. After last night, she didn't want to listen to either.

Her phone rang. She took it out of her purse. When she saw Chuck's name, she answered it, holding it against her ear. He'd heard about what had happened, and she told him not to worry. The worst was over, and he and Raine should stay in California until the date they'd originally planned to return.

"What's this going to do to the reputation of the B and B?" he asked.

"Who knows? It might bring more guests. People are ghoulish. But I don't know if that's the right question."

"What's that?"

"The right question is, do you want to run a bed-and-breakfast? I don't."

"Mom, you cut to the chase."

"That's me. The cutter." *Or the shooter.*

"To be honest, I'm going to be busy during tourist season with the Art Mart, and Raine will be busy with her music."

"Honey, it's okay to say no. I've done the B and B for enough years. We could sell it. Or you and Raine could live in it."

"Are you going to marry Nate?"

She glanced at Nate, but he was still facing forward. "I'll tell you when or if we make that decision."

"I worry about you."

"It's payback. I worried about you for more than thirty years."

He laughed. "You're not giving me any answers."

"When I have answers, I'll give them to you. For now, well, I'm alive." Her voice rose, and she looked at Nate again. As if he felt her gaze, he glanced at her, too. "I'm alive and I have a cat."

"And marriage," Chuck said. "What about that?"

"Oops. We're here now. Talk to you later." She hung up as Nate pulled into the resort's driveway. Perfect timing, she thought as she tucked her phone in her purse and took a look at the prettiest resort in the area. Even with snow on the trees and the Lake Michigan waters still and icy.

They were staying in a villa in the back of the resort. August had told her last night, his tone firm, that she was a part of the family, and she was there as a guest. Sylvia was not a crier, but she'd been sniffing back tears. Nearly getting murdered by a pair of serial killers had that effect on her.

She stood tall now, walking into the villa, taking off her coat, and hanging it in the small closet in the hall. Because that's what she did. Acted as if everything was all right.

Nate hung up his jacket, too. He wasn't as neat as she was, but he wasn't a slob.

Then his hands clasped hers.

"You know," she whispered and glanced sideways at him.

"That you've killed before?" He shrugged one shoulder. "I didn't know for sure. I guessed."

"Aren't you afraid?"

"You would never shoot me."

Tears sprouted from her eyes. She was turning into a crybaby. But she kept her spine straight and turned around to face him.

"Because of you," he said, "a sick serial killer will no longer kill."

She sucked in a breath. "Do you want to know about the others?"

"Not really."

"I will never shoot you." She took a deep breath. "I thought I had reasons to kill before. I wish now that I wouldn't have." But she frowned, knowing she'd just lied to him. Her first instinct when she even suspected something wasn't right last night had been to put a loaded gun in her pocket.

But this really was the last time. If she continued doing things like this, there would be a ridiculous amount of dead people in Door County. Perhaps Dane County, too, since she and Nate were living in Madison now. Especially during election years.

She took a deep breath. Of course, she wouldn't go crazy like that. And it wasn't as if she was one of the Avengers, fighting crime with a superpower. She was just a middle-aged woman who didn't want to go to jail.

The killing stopped now.

"I'm not the same person I used to be." She stood with her spine straight. "You didn't have to say that you killed Brad."

"It's not a bad thing." His eyes twinkled. "People admire me. I'm a hero."

Her spine relaxed, and she snorted. "So that's why you're taking credit."

"I'll write a screenplay. Make myself a hero."

"I've always wanted to marry a hero."

He stilled, but his eyes lit up. "Seriously?"

"Serious as the grave." She smiled at him, and her heart felt like it was expanding. This man who was funny and smart and kind—and good in bed—had stolen her heart. Or, rather, she was giving it to him gladly.

This man, her Jewish lover, was also her Christmas miracle. He knew what and who she was. He guessed what she'd done, and yet he still trusted her. He still loved her. He still wanted to marry her.

"We could have been murdered by a crazy person yesterday," she said. "These last couple years, well, a lot of craziness has happened."

"You want me to keep you from the crazy?"

"I don't think you can stop the crazy." She gazed into his brown eyes. "I think we're both a little crazy. But I love your crazy."

"I love your crazy, too." He stepped closer.

She put her hands out, and he stopped. "You know that Teela comes with me?" she asked.

"Of course she does." His smile widened. "After all, she's the real hero of this story."

Sylvia laughed even as he kissed her. Life was precious and could be over in a flash. It had taken her too long to figure out what her role in life was, but now she knew: a cat mom, and a soon-to-be wife to the best man she knew.

At her feet, Teela weaved against her ankles, and her heart that had felt empty for so long was filled with love.

Thank you!

Thanks for reading *Christmas Redemption*. I'm having so much fun writing this series, and I hope you're enjoying reading the books. Reviews are appreciated.

I'm working on my next *Love & Murder* book now. To be notified when it or other books are available, sign up to my new release email list at:

www.edieramer.com/newsletter-sign-up.

Special Thanks

I appreciate my copy editor, Amy Knupp at Blue Otter Editing, more than she knows. She's not only a great editor, she's also evilly funny. And huge thanks to Judy at Judicious Revisions for catching little errors that I always seem to miss, though when I send the manuscript to her, I think it's perfect. Both these ladies are the best!

About the Author

A *USA Today* bestselling author, **Edie Ramer** is funnier on the page than in real life. She writes stories with heart, attitude, suspense, and sometimes humor. She lives in Wisconsin with her husband and one very important cat. She's happy to be able to do what she loves nearly every day, and she loves hearing from readers.

http://edieramer.com/